Master of D.E.A.T.H.

Directorate for Espionage, Assassination, Terrorism and Harassment

He's in the business of suppressing freedom, starting wars and murdering innocents—all for power. And money.

You won't find him in the directory. He'll find you.

Now available in the exciting new series
from Gold Eagle Books

TRACK

by Jerry Ahern

TRACK

Master of D.E.A.T.H.

JERRY AHERN

A GOLD EAGLE BOOK FROM
W☉RLDWIDE

TORONTO · NEW YORK · LONDON · PARIS
AMSTERDAM · STOCKHOLM · HAMBURG
ATHENS · MILAN · TOKYO · SYDNEY

For Stan Hodsdon—
hunter, outdoorsman and all-around good guy.
All the best, my friend.

———————————◆———————————

First edition June 1985

ISBN 0-373-62007-1

Printed in Canada

PROLOGUE

"Read me the clipping." It was cold with the lid of the coffin-shaped tanning booth raised.

"All right," he said, clearing his throat. "Bonn, West Germany, November 3. Informed Western sources here today disavowed any knowledge of reports filtering from the Soviet Union regarding the group called by the British press "the Vindicators." They are allegedly a highly trained and well-equipped fighting unit, contrary to vehement denials by Soviet officials and in the Soviet press. The group reportedly is wreaking havoc on Soviet police, paramilitary and intelligence operations inside the Soviet Union. First reports of the Vindicators originated from the official news agency of the People's Republic of China, involving an allegedly successful raid on a Soviet military-scientific facility near Alma Ata in Soviet Kazakhstan. A high-ranking United States government source who refused to be identified claimed that the facility near Alma Ata was the focal point of Soviet research into mind control, remote viewing and telekinesis.

"Within weeks of the reported raid at Alma Ata, a second commando strike allegedly took place at Karaganda, involving a Soviet missile-guidance-system development center. In rapid succession, attacks took place in or near Sverdlovsk, Orenburg, Kirovo-Chepetsk, Uglich and Yegoryevsk. At Yegoryevsk, on the very outskirts of Moscow, a Soviet army intelligence training facility was rumored to have been completely destroyed as the result of bombings and a fire. The Soviet news agency Tass reported the incident as resulting from a defective boiler and labeled damage to the facility 'extensive.' American diplomatic sources in Moscow expressed official regret but had no further comment.

"Privately, Soviet officials seem worried. It is rumored that the Vindicators have been at least tentatively identified. The team purportedly consists of five men, one of whom may be black and at least one of them is almost certainly Russian. Sometime before the first incident involving the psychic-research facility near Alma Ata, rumors ran rampant that a highly placed officer in the Committee for State Security, better known as the KGB, was the subject of a nationwide search throughout the Soviet Union. Rumors persist that this unidentified KGB official was never captured."

He cleared his throat again. "That's it."

"What additional information do we have?"

"This could be the work of a man by the name of Daniel Track. Ex-major in the U.S. Army Criminal Investigation Division, a specialist in counterterrorist techniques, SWAT training—stuff like that. This man Track went to work for Sir Abner Chesterton at the Consortium of International Insurance Underwriters. But he disappeared after a gunfight in Atlanta and was rumored to have gone to India. He hasn't surfaced.''

"Who else?''

"Okay,'' he said as he lit a cigarette, clearing his throat once again. "Track worked with his nephew, George Beegh—''

"George B. what?''

"No, B-e-e-g-h—that's the man's last name. George Beegh had six years in Air Force intelligence and left with a good service record. He joined his uncle and also went to work for the Consortium. It appears that Track, Beegh and Sir Abner Chesterton became rather close.''

"What's this man's background, this Chesterton?''

"During World War II—yeah, I got it here.'' He shuffled his paperwork. It was difficult to do as he stood there trying not to look into the tanning booth. "Chesterton's knighthood is hereditary, dating from Queen Victoria's time. Chesterton was one of the youngest men ever accepted in the Royal Commandos during World War II. After that, he served for ten years in British Secret Intelligence Service, and there's some evidence to suggest that he was part of the old-boy network for a long time after that. He was the chief coordinator for the Consortium with Interpol and other world police and intelligence agencies, in charge of major crime and terrorism. And he's dropped out of sight, just like Track and Beegh.''

"How about the black?''

"That's an interesting one. Track's had a long-standing affair with Desiree Goth—''

"The gunrunner and smuggler?" a surprised voice asked.

He cleared his throat again, not knowing what to do with the ashes from his cigarette, holding it carefully. "She could be supplying them with weapons and explosives," he suggested.

"Never mind about that. Tell me about the black."

"He's Desiree Goth's assistant, and it seems likely he's also her bodyguard. He's been with her at least since she got into smuggling in the Mediterranean and probably before that, as well. He's called Zulu, and nobody seems to know any other name for him. His place of birth is some village with an unpronounceable name in what was at the time the Belgian Congo."

"What's the ID on the Russian the clipping talked about?"

"He's a friend of Track's, a major in the KGB named Sergei Baslovitch. Career officer in the KGB, one of their best overseas operatives, if not the best." The ashes from his cigarette fell on top of his shoes, but he didn't brush them off onto the Oriental rug. "It seems pretty clear that Track, Beegh, Chesterton, Baslovitch and this black man, Zulu, are the ones the newspapers are calling the Vindicators."

"Why did you bother me with this?"

"Well, if these five men with the help of this arms dealer Desiree Goth can hit the KGB and the Soviet army right where they live—"

"Well?"

"If they ever found out about the existence of the Directorate—"

"You don't actually suppose five men and a woman—"

"Two women. A russian scientist named Dr. Tatiana Ivanova was arrested shortly after the raid on the psychic-research center near Alma Ata. She must be linked to them because the first attack after that resulted in her being freed. And she hasn't surfaced, either."

"Five men and two women, then. The point is, you don't suppose they could have even the slightest impact on me."

The man shrugged. "I thought we might want to keep an eye on them. Just to be on the safe side. They seem very effective."

"All right. But let them play their games in Russia. It can't hurt. If they resurface in the West, have them eliminated. Is there anything else about them?"

"No, nothing."

"Close the lid of the tanning booth on the way out. And don't get those ashes on the carpet."

"Yes, yes, of course." He closed the lid. It was hard not to look, closing the lid like that.

1

He had practiced with the ninja climbing spikes specifically for this. The claws secured to his hands and feet scratched against the concrete of the wall as he moved, but the scratching sounds would be impossible to detect at any distance. At least that's what Dan Track told himself.

He stopped as he heard the movement on the wall above him. He held his breath, hanging there from the four claws, perhaps forty feet above the concrete apron. Track breathed deeply under the black scarf bound over the lower portion of his face, feeling it suck inward as he inhaled.

Above him, there was movement again, and he heard the sound diminishing.

After a moment, Track started upward. He was less than fifteen feet from the top of the wall. Looking to his right, he saw George Beegh a few yards below him, but climbing steadily. Turning his head to the other side, he saw Sergei Baslovitch. Both his nephew and the Russian wore the same uniform he did—black tabby boots, loose-fitting trousers bound at the knees and ankles, a loose-fitting shirt bound at the waist, a scarf covering the lower face beneath the black camouflage makeup, a scarf bound over the hair and tied at the nape of the neck and gloves of close-fitting cloth—all in dull matte black. Each man had a Walther MPK 9mm submachine gun slung on his back. Walther P-5 9mm pistols in specially built holsters designed to accommodate a silencer were strapped to their waists. Each man also carried six stainless-steel *shuriken* throwing spikes on the backs of their gloves.

Beneath the black clothing, each man had a personal gun and knife: George had his Smith & Wesson 469 minigun and a Puma lockblade folding hunter; Baslovitch had an HK P-7 9mm and a Puma lockblade; and Track had a Detonics Pocket 9 double-action stainless-steel 9mm. He, too, carried one of the Puma lockblade folding hunters.

Track peered over the lip of the facility wall as he reached the top. The guard he had heard stood about twenty feet away, back turned. Track heard the sound of a lighter being worked, and as the man lit a cigarette Track rolled over the wall into a standing position. Tugging the claws from his feet and hands, he reached into one of the pouches of his utility belt for an SAS commando saw and the two wooden pegs. He slipped the pegs through the rings at each end of the wire saw and crept forward.

He could smell the smoke of the man's cigarette. Ten feet.

Track quickened his pace, his concentration focused beyond the man he was going to silence.

Track snaked the loop over the man's head, his fists tightening on the pegs, and drew the saw around the neck of the guard. Wheeling to his left, Track pulled the man's body up against his shoulder. The wire of the saw sliced cleanly through skin, tissue and muscle.

As he eased the body downward, Track twisted the Commando saw free of the flesh and cartilage of the neck, running it once across the chest of the dead man's uniform to clean away some of the blood before he returned it to its pouch. Taking his silenced Walther P-5 into his fist, he crouched in the shadow where he had placed the body of the guard.

Baslovitch rolled over the wall, and Track nodded to the Russian as the former KGB major moved away from Track to find his own cover.

Then George came over the lip of the wall, rolled into a crouch and stripped away his climbing claws. In an instant, Baslovitch was beside George.

George held his silenced Walther in his right fist, the pistol moving back and forth along the guard catwalk on the top of the wall like a wand, searching the shadow for danger.

Baslovitch's Walther was also drawn, and together he and George moved toward Track's position, Baslovitch looking back, his pistol aimed into the night, George aiming down to the compound beyond the wall.

When they got beside Track, they pulled up. Track gestured with his pistol toward the guard and then the three men started ahead, keeping close to the wall. Track held his pistol in his fist, his fingers closed tight on it like a vise.

TATIANA, CHESTERTON THOUGHT, was perfect for the part since Russian was her native language. But the black wig she wore over her blond hair was most unbecoming. She had penciled her eyebrows darker to match the wig, and the effect was to give her face an almost hollow look when compared to the radiant good health her countenance normally exuded.

"We are coming to the gate now. Be silent," Tatiana murmured. Chesterton lowered the lid of his coffin and lay still, holding the Walther MPJ in both fists across his chest. If the coffin was opened, the game would be up, and silence would be useless. In fact, it might even prove valuable to make all the racket possible, distracting attention from Track, George and Baslovitch on the compound wall.

He wondered what Zulu thought in the coffin beside him in the van.

Sir Abner Chesterton realized he was holding his breath and he started to breathe again. The smell of the fresh pine of the coffin in which he lay was slightly nauseating.

Bringing coffins to Beria prison outside Leningrad was no oddity. Tatiana had, with George aiding her, observed Beria prison for two weeks to construct schedules of guard tours, deliveries and removals.

Chesterton thought of George Beegh. Finding out that his father, Robert Beegh, had been murdered and that his mother had been doomed by a Russian agent had taken an incredible toll on the young man.

But to George's credit, on all the missions they had undertaken since penetrating Soviet territory again after the raid near Alma Ata, George had been noth-

ing but professional. Chesterton had seen men consumed with blood lust for vengeance, consumed to
the point where reason had no meaning, where effi-
ciency and success of the operation were only secondary to the kill.

If anything, George had become more efficient,
but Chesterton wondered how long the young American could go on. Every man has his breaking point.
Thankfully this was to be the last mission.

With a squeal of brakes the truck stopped, and
Chesterton held his breath again. It would be the
guard station at the wall where Tatiana would show
the counterfeit identification papers Baslovitch had
manufactured.

Chesterton forced himself to concentrate on something other than what might be transpiring between
Tatiana and the guards as she delivered the con-
signment of three coffins. Through documents stolen
during the raid at Uglich, Baslovitch had learned
the code name of the top Soviet agent in North
America.

Potempkin, the controller.

Chesterton considered this. There was also mention of a person Baslovitch had known, a woman
code-named Hummingbird, courier and top agent
beneath Potempkin.

To get these two would end the war Dan Track had
declared against the KGB—at least for now. Already
arrangements were being made in Mexico. But Mexico was a long way from the dark and cold environs of
Leningrad. A long way.

The truck started up again and Chesterton

breathed deeply. The smell of the pine wood of the coffin in which he lay still nauseated him.

THE SPECIALLY MODIFIED Hind-D helicopter had started out in England for a British SIS mission that had apparently never come off. Built at the factory of Mikhail Mill in Russia, it had been shot down in Pakistan during a Soviet raid across the border from Afghanistan. The British had been so eager to have it that Desiree Goth had felt almost obliged to get it for them, and felt not a whit of guilt at selling it to them for an even five hundred thousand U.S. dollars. But then the mission the British had planned after having the machine painstakingly restored by a team of automobile and aircraft restoration experts had been cancelled. They had asked her if she wished to buy the helicopter back and she had agreed, since she had been looking for just such a machine. She had given them a good price for the fully restored craft—four hundred thousand dollars. She had inquired who was to fly the craft for the SIS endeavor and been given the name of the Japanese mercenary. She had paid him the twenty-five thousand dollars that the British were to have paid him, and now had an aircraft, a pilot and was seventy-five thousand dollars to the good.

She spoke to Hideo. "I will now tell you exactly where we are going, Hideo."

The Japanese man looked at her across the gray card table in the far corner of the hangar she had obtained. Hideo smiled. "Let me guess, Miss Desiree—Russia?"

Desiree smiled back, then lit a cigarette. She stood, thrusting her left hand into the side pocket of the heavy tweed midcalf-length skirt she wore, and listened to the heels of her boots click against the concrete as she walked to the dirt-smudged window. She stared out onto the wet night that closed about the airfield. "You are very perceptive. When this is finished, I could use a man of your abilities. The money would be better than you get now and the work less dangerous—most of the time, at any event."

"I'm your man, Miss Desiree," Hideo replied cheerfully.

She smiled at that—he wasn't her man. He might well become her employee, ferrying aircraft for her from one nation to another, but he wasn't her man. Her man was across the waters of the Gulf of Finland and doing something terribly dangerous right now.

She turned away from the window, dropping the cigarette to the floor, crushing it under the sole of her right boot. "This is the most important mission I have ever hired someone to perform, Hideo. If all goes well, there will be an extra twenty-five thousand dollars in it for you."

"These must be important men."

"Yes." She smiled. "Very important, Hideo. Very important to me."

She glanced at her watch beneath the cuff of her black sweater and then stared out the window. "Very important," she whispered to the darkness and the cold rain beyond the smudged glass.

DAN TRACK WATCHED from the shadows as the van crossed the compound's square and slowed before the entrance to the Environmental Research Unit. He hated euphemisms with a passion. Environmental Research Unit translated to experimentation on human subjects concerning the effects of nerve gas and biological agents. If a compound proved effective here, it would be field-tested under direction of the army or the KGB—field-tested on massive numbers of human beings in Afghanistan and perhaps elsewhere.

The call had been placed from the Environmental Research Unit to the coffin manufacturer's factory—the coffin manufacturer was a member of the Resistance, a Jew who would now go underground despite Track's offer to take the man out with him. The offer had been refused.

As Track thought of the look in the man's eyes, the Resistance fighter's words came back to him, "Others of my people cannot leave, do not have freedom, are persecuted, hunted. I, too, shall stay."

The truck, the driver's uniform Tatiana wore and the three coffins would damn the coffin maker for the rest of his life with the Soviet authorities. But the man's wife was dead, his oldest daughter dead, his youngest daughter and eldest son escaped to freedom in the West. His youngest son would go with him into the underground.

The truck stopped, and Track watched as Tatiana stepped down from the driver's compartment.

She walked ahead, into the receiving area of the research unit. The coffins were customarily carried in through the front door; what became of them afterward was conjecture. But Track assumed they were accumulated and then taken out in the large Ural semitrailer truck that left the facility once a week and drove into the countryside to the Forensic Sciences Research Station. What happened afterward, why coffins were used rather than rubber or canvas bags, Track had never learned.

Tatiana reemerged. Two guards walking with her had AKMs slung across their stomachs.

She opened the rear doors of the vans, whistling a few bars of "Hey, Andruska"—it was a code signal to Sir Abner Chesterton and Zulu that the guards were with her and all went according to plan.

As she climbed into the rear of the van, her gray coveralls tightened over her little rear end, Track glanced to Baslovitch flanking him on the left and raised his eyebrows. Baslovitch elbowed him in the ribs.

Track looked back to Tatiana. She had disappeared inside the truck, and the whistling had stopped.

In an instant, she reappeared at the rear of the truck, and the guards came closer to her as she beckoned them. Their rifles were across their backs now, and as they drew level with her, her hands snapped toward their faces.

At that moment, Track was up and moving. George and Baslovitch were beside him. Ahead, the two guards were grasping their throats, staggering backward as two black-clad figures—Chesterton and Zulu—leaped from the back of the van.

Track dropped to the ground and rolled under the truck as Zulu and Chesterton hauled the two dead guards back inside the van and closed the doors. George was already beneath the truck, and they were soon joined by Baslovitch.

A panel in the undercarriage of the truck opened, and Track heard Zulu's rasping whisper, "Major!"

Track reached up, and the familiar shape of the SPAS-12 came into his hands. Zulu then handed down an AKM for Baslovitch and another AKM for George.

Track knocked once on the truck's undercarriage and rolled out from beneath the van. As he got to his feet, he worked off the carrying safety on the SPAS shotgun, leaving only the quick employment safety set at the front of the trigger guard.

As George tapped him on the back, he started ahead, pulling up to the right of the double doors leading into the Environmental Research Unit. George was beside him, while Baslovitch took a position to the left of the doors.

There was a moment when nothing happened, then Tatiana, garbed in black ninja gear like the rest of them now, rolled out from beneath the truck, followed by Chesterton and Zulu.

Soon they were six—three on each side of the doors.

Track gave the signal, and he and Zulu, brandishing silenced Walthers, stepped in front of the doors, grabbed the handles and pulled.

As they rushed inside, the heat of the building hit them like a wall. A uniformed guard rose from his seat by the door while another guard reached across his desk to a communications console.

Track shot the second man between the eyes. To his left, Zulu fired a killing shot square into the first guard's forehead.

As Track vaulted the guardrail, he saw Zulu running ahead to the end of the small reception room, hiding beside the doorway, the Walther muzzle up, ready.

Track checked each guard for signs of life and then looked back toward the door—Chesterton, George, Baslovitch and Tatiana were already inside.

Baslovitch had worked with Tatiana over the months spent in the Soviet Union, teaching her the use of weapons and sharpening her skill in the martial arts. It was her first mission with them, and Baslovitch had promised never to leave her side.

Track had laughingly told him how self-sacrificing it was to stay with the woman he was in love with, so close that they could touch. The Russian had frowned a moment and then laughed.

As Track crossed through the swinging gate, George and Chesterton were busy propping up the dead guards in their chairs, slapping adhesive over the wounds.

The bodies were swiveled in their chairs to face away from the doorway.

Track caught up with Zulu beside the door leading deeper into the building. He dropped into a crouch and turned the door handle lightly as George, Baslovitch and Tatiana fell in behind him. George peered through the crack. For three weeks the basic elements of the raid had been rehearsed. For one week, nine hours a day, the raid had been rehearsed in detail.

George tapped Track on the shoulder—all clear. Track swung the door back and George and Chesterton raced silently through, their pistols held ready.

Baslovitch and Tatiana followed, then Track went through, and as he looked back he saw Zulu pull the door closed behind them.

They were in a long, bare corridor, painted an institutional green. George and Chesterton ran ahead, while Tatiana and Baslovitch walked down each side. Track and Zulu covered the rear.

Track heard a door open farther along the hallway and wheeled toward the sound. But Baslovitch already had the man, his folding knife ripping across the lab-coated man's throat. Blood spouted from the artery, and Tatiana shrunk back for an instant before ramming a gloved hand forward over the man's mouth to stifle any scream that might escape. Baslovitch disappeared inside the doorway for an instant, dragging the body inside after him. When he reappeared, he held a cloth in his hand and used it to wipe the blood off the linoleum-tiled floor. Working quickly, he threw the bedsheet through the open doorway and then closed the door soundlessly.

Baslovitch and Tatiana started ahead, and Track looked past them to see George and Chesterton already in position behind the next set of doors. According to the coffin maker, the guard who usually sat on the other side of the door spent most of his time drooling over an American girlie magazine he kept underneath a few papers clipped to his clipboard.

Track hoped the guard was looking at something good—it would be the last thing he enjoyed.

Track moved faster now, breaking into a run, passing Baslovitch and Tatiana, leaving Zulu on drag alone.

Chesterton opened the right-hand door, and Track thrust the right half of his body through it as the guard looked up from his clipboard. Reacting in a split second, Track snapped one of the *shuriken* throwing spikes forward. The spike penetrated the guard's skull in the middle of the forehead, and the man's head snapped back into space then recoiled forward, sagging over the clipboard.

Track was through the door, his pistol back in his right fist. He glanced at the guard. The guard's nose was pressed flat against the crotch of a redhead, the redhead getting redder by the second as blood oozed over the centerfold.

"What a way to go," Track murmured under his breath.

He walked past the guard and peered through an open doorway. In front of him, a catwalk circumscribed a sunken laboratory facility. The laboratory was as big as a football field, and the distance from floor to ceiling was about thirty feet. Steel stairways wound down in spirals from the catwalk to the laboratory floor.

White-coated men and women were at work everywhere. On one table was a body, completely blue.

Off to one side a man struggled in a fog-filled

booth, hammering his fists against unbreakable glass as the fog grew more dense. Finally the hammering stopped. The man and woman who had observed him die attended to their clipboards unemotionally.

Track edged back.

He was glad he had come.

2

After Dan Track had viewed the lab layout, they had split up as planned. Track, Zulu, Baslovitch and Tatiana waited outside the double doors for the required four minutes. Chesterton and George ran into the side corridor that led to the cell section of Beria prison.

Only three men were known to be currently held there. But in addition to these three, men and women were continually brought to the prison for use in the KGB's experiments.

George ran now, the Walther P-5 with its brand X silencer in his right fist, Sir Abner Chesterton despite his almost sixty years keeping pace with him.

The corridor took a bend right as it followed the shape of the laboratory.

George checked his watch. It was two minutes before his uncle would start the attack.

George quickened his pace along the hall until he reached the third door on the right, a ladies' lounge. He tried the door—locked as it should be.

George reached into the pouch on his utility belt and extracted a PCS lock-pick set. He drew one of the picks with certainty and inserted it into the lock mechanism, twisting it upward slightly, then left, then down, then applying pressure to the right.

He turned the doorknob and the door opened. Chesterton raced through, the Walther held ready in his right fist.

George glanced up and down the corridor once, then followed Chesterton into the room, silently closed the door and locked it.

Chesterton was already stripping away the two ninja scarves that masked his face and hair, then the utility belt, then the tabby boots. George looked around the room—a faded blue couch was against one wall, and on a low table sat copies of *Soviet Life* and an ashtray half overflowing with lipstick-stained filter-tip cigarettes.

One wall was broken by a doorway, and stalls were visible beyond.

George looked back at Chesterton. Soviet army boots were out of the backpack Chesterton wore, and Chesterton had stripped off the black pants and top of the ninja outfit, revealing a KGB guard uniform he wore beneath it.

Chesterton smiled, whispering hoarsely, "I just hope you and your uncle appreciate my shaving my mustache and getting this ridiculously short haircut, George." And Chesterton settled the uniform cap on his head and picked up his rifle.

George was already caching the ninja gear in Chesterton's pack, slinging it over his shoulder.

When George looked up, Chesterton was stuffing the silenced Walther beneath his tunic. The Englishman's face creased with a smile. "Let's go, George. I can't stand this uniform hat—too bloody tight." Chesterton was at the door.

George unlocked it and opened it a crack, peering into the corridor. His eyes met no one.

He nodded to Chesterton, and the Englishman slid through.

George looked at his watch—less than a minute to go before the shooting would start and the alarms would sound.

George waited.

Sir Abner Chesterton had never really considered his Russian all that marvelous, but he felt confident in his speech—Tatiana and Baslovitch both had tutored him on the right inflections and the right pronunciations. And the universal truism was proven again—Chesterton smiled thinking of it, walking along the corridor toward the guard station beyond the bend. If a woman taught a man how to speak a foreign language, the man would often find himself being laughed at for the way he spoke it, however excellent. And Chesterton supposed the reverse was true, as well.

He turned the corridor and stopped. From the diagram the Resistance agent had supplied, the guard post had seemed farther along the corridor. In Russian, Chesterton began his rehearsed speech. "I have just been given word, Comrade Corporal that the terrorists called the Vindicators have invaded the compound and have disabled the alarm system. They are suspected to be coming this way to attempt to free the prisoners. I will wait with you." And without waiting for a response, without answering the quizzical looks as to his identity, with prideful military precision, he slung his rifle forward and began to cover the corridor.

The two genuine Soviet guards rose from their desk and the one took up his assault rifle, the other drawing a Tokarev automatic from a flap holster at his waist.

George would be coming, making some telltale noise to alert them.

Chesterton heard the clang of something metallic against the wall in the corridor beyond the bend. Chesterton, snapped, "They are coming!"

Both guards took a step forward, and Chesterton let the AKM fall on its sling, drawing his silencer-fitted P-5.

The silencer caught in the waistband of his trousers.

One of the guards was beginning to turn around.

Chesterton yelled, "George!"

Both guards spun toward Chesterton, but with the P-5 free now, Chesterton fired, killing one with a shot into the neck. Swiveling the pistol toward the second man he prepared to fire, but the man's eyes suddenly went wide and the body quivered, then quivered again.

The body fell forward, and as Chesterton stepped clear he saw two *shuriken* spikes in the back of the man's neck at the top of the spine.

Chesterton looked up. George was already running past him.

Chesterton threw off his military cap—it was giving him a headache. He picked up the keys from the pistol-armed dead guard, throwing the pistol one way along the corridor floor, the magazine in the other direction.

He raced after George along the corridor carrying the extra AKM.

Double doors stood at the end of the hallway—imposing steel doors this time, and locked.

Chesterton skidded to a halt beside George, handing his young American friend the liberated AKM. George stripped the magazine from it, then began partial disassembly to render it inoperable.

The second before Chesterton found the right key and placed it to the lock, the sirens began to wail.

He wrenched open the double doors, stepping aside, the clatter of George's Walther MPK submachine gun deafening in the confined space of the doorway, but three men armed with AKMs went down on the other side of the doors.

Chesterton snatched the ninja mask from his pack and covered his face with the black scarf as he ran after George.

3

Dan Track held the SPAS-12 tensioned on its sling in his right fist, working the trigger in and out, the buckshot peppering the KGB technical staff in the laboratory beneath him as he ran the catwalk. The Walther MPK was in his left fist, and 3-round bursts burped from the subgun into targets of opportunity. Returning fire was coming from the floor of the laboratory, mixed with screams and shouts of pain.

Track looked back once. Zulu stood on the opposite end of the catwalk, hosing his subgun into the mass of now-fleeing laboratory workers. Baslovitch and Tatiana were starting down one of the spiraling metal stairways toward the laboratory floor.

Track fired the last two rounds from the SPAS-12, killing one of the white-coated technicians as she shoved another of the helpless victims—this one strapped at neck, chest, waist and ankles, to a gurney—into a cylindrical glass container.

The woman fell, but another of the KGB technicians slammed closed the door of the cylinder.

Track let the empty SPAS fall to his side, swinging the MPK forward, waiting, killing the technician. But the door was shut.

A block and tackle were suspended from the center

of the laboratory ceiling, the chain end hooked along the rail of the catwalk.

Track ran for it, firing the last burst from the Walther subgun into one of the uniformed KGB guards. The sirens were wailing deafeningly loud now.

Grabbing the chain, he swung his right leg over the rail, then his left and sat perched on the edge.

A uniformed KGB guard charged toward him, and Track snatched one of the *shuriken* throwing spikes from the back of his left glove and snapped it through the air into the man's chest.

Then Track grasped the two lengths of chain and swung down to the laboratory floor, his feet crashing against the head and neck of one of the technicians, hammering the body forward into the wall of the glass cylinder.

Track kicked himself away from the far wall, swinging out again on the pendulum of chain, his feet striking one of the uniformed KGB guards now emerging into the laboratory. There seemed to be dozens of them. The guard's body flew right and Track released the chain, twisting his body in midair, and slammed down on a gurney. As the gurney shot off across the laboratory floor, Track snatched another *shuriken* spike from his glove and hurled it into the throat of another of the guards.

Track rolled from the gurney to the floor, his elbow smashing through a glass-fronted cabinet, one of the technicians smashing a large glass beaker toward his head, Track's foot snapping up into the man's crotch. As the technician doubled over,

Track's foot kicked against the base of the nose, breaking the bone, driving it up and through the eth-moid bone, the eyes wide open in death as the technician collapsed.

Another of the uniformed KGB guards. Track freed his elbow and rolled right, banging his ribs on the emptied SPAS-12, snatching another of the *shuri-ken* spikes, hurling it into the forehead of the uniformed guard.

Track was up on his feet, dumping the empty magazine for the MPK, grasping a fresh one from one of the three magazine pouches on his utility belt, ramming it home.

Track wheeled left, and two pistol-armed guards rushed him.

He fired the MPK, dropping both men.

He started for the cylindrical glass container and the prisoner on the gurney. One of the technicians was moving toward an array of large, multicolored buttons. Track fired the MPK, the man's body stumbling forward as both hands clasped the small of the back.

Track rammed the butt of the subgun into the cylinder's hermetically sealed door, throwing open the doorway after reaching inside to free the lock. He dragged the gurney out but the man strapped to its bed was already dead, stray gunshots peppering his rib cage.

Track turned, firing the Walther in frustration. Zulu ran down one of the spiral staircases near the entrance, a subgun in one hand, a Walther P-5 in the other, both weapons firing.

Track rammed a fresh magazine home and fired a 3-round burst into the neck of another of the guards.

Baslovitch and Tatiana were down to the floor now, hosing their subguns toward the door through which more of the uniformed KGB guards were pouring.

Track ran across the laboratory floor, skipping over bodies of dead technicians and guards, running toward Baslovitch and Tatiana. Joining them, he emptied the subgun's magazine into the open doorway. Bodies fell, piling on top of one another. Some of the KGB personnel took cover behind their dead comrades, firing back.

Track edged around the corner of the doorway, Tatiana beside him, Baslovitch on the opposite side.

The Walther empty, Track rammed the last fresh magazine home, shaking his head toward Baslovitch to indicate that he was not ready.

He started feeding buckshot into the tube of the SPAS-12, filling the magazine, then working the magazine cut-off and chambering a ninth round. He worked off the quick employment safety, then shouted to Baslovitch, "Now!"

Track wheeled into the doorway, working the trigger of the SPAS as fast as he could. To his left, Tatiana fired her MPK. On his right stood Baslovitch, an MPK in the one fist, a P-5 in the other.

A voice boomed from behind them, "Everybody down!"

Track threw himself to the floor, against the nearer of the dead guards, dragging Tatiana to the floor with him as Baslovitch hurled himself to the right.

Subgun fire and assault-rifle fire poured over their heads as Track rolled onto his back, feeding fresh rounds into the magazine tube of the SPAS. As he got to his knees, he could see Zulu firing in fury.

Track emptied the SPAS through the doorway. Prone beside him, Tatiana fired her subgun. Baslovitch filled the air with lead from his MPK.

The smell of gunpowder was stifling. The moans of dead men filled the air. But the sirens wailed on.

Track was feeding the magazine tube of the hungry SPAS as he got to his feet.

He glanced over his shoulder and saw Zulu towering behind him at the approximate center of the laboratory, the Walther in his left fist, an AKM in his right.

All about him, as Track's eyes surveyed the carnage over the edge of the black ninja scarf that masked his face, was death.

Tatiana had started across the room, Baslovitch at her side, gathering documents scattered over the laboratory floor, some of them dripping blood, and securing them in a case under her shoulder.

Track, with Zulu beside him, started climbing the hill of bodies that blocked the door from the laboratory. They weren't done yet.

4

George raced along the corridor as more guards ran up. He tucked back as one-handed, he sprayed the MPK along the corridor's length. Chesterton was opposite him now in the KGB uniform and boots but with a black ninja scarf masking his face.

Chunks of wall blew out around him, and George reached into the bag at his side for a fragmentation grenade.

He pulled the pin, letting the handle fly as he tossed the grenade down the corridor, tucking back as it detonated and chunks of plaster and ceiling tile crashed down. Smoke belched along the hallway, and George shielded his head with his hands and arms as he dropped to one knee and crouched.

And then he was up, running, a fresh magazine going up the well of the MPK, firing it in 3-round bursts, jumping the bodies of the fragged guards, Chesterton beside him. Chesterton's MPK and AKM fired in staccato bursts.

Another set of double doors, but no locking mechanism.

George glanced toward Chesterton, and the Englishman nodded.

George's foot snapped out, the doors opening inward, swinging fast, George firing a burst from the Walther subgun, then throwing himself down and away as Chesterton rolled a grenade through the open doorway. The answering fire from behind the doorway was suddenly gone, and in its place were a belching of smoke and a shower of debris.

George ran through the doorway, Chesterton beside him.

A guard raised his head from behind an overturned desk, the desk smoldering, papers burning on the floor.

George made to fire, but Chesterton fired first, a 3-round burst from the subgun can-opening the man's forehead, the body slamming back, the head a bloody pulp as it cracked against the back wall.

George stopped, feeding a fresh magazine to the MPK. Chesterton did the same, throwing down his AKM. "Damned thing's empty, anyway," the Englishman murmured.

George started walking toward the three cells at the far end of the corridor.

One of the faces he saw in one of the cells made him start to run.

TRACK AND ZULU had crossed the covered walkway between the research unit and the prison facility where test subjects were kept for weeks or months or sometimes only days before their use in the KGB's experiments. They both ran, Zulu calling out as they neared the doors, "You are aware that they may have executed their test subjects?"

Track only nodded in reply.

When they reached the doors they were locked, but the men had come prepared. Zulu plastered thin strips of plastique at the midjoint, then squished a blasting cap into the middle of each strip and ran back.

Track already had the MPK on line, firing two 3-round bursts at the plastique strips, throwing himself down as the doors exploded. Chunks of steel, pieces of plaster and hunks of ceiling tile sprayed along the corridor.

"Al! right?" Track yelled.

"Quite!" Zulu replied.

Track was up then, Zulu running beside him, their subguns spraying beyond the doorways, through the smoke, as they jumped through.

Dead guards lay everywhere, brick-sized shards of jagged steel penetrating torsos and heads.

Track and Zulu methodically checked each body, picking up usable weapons.

"Here!"

Track looked up, running toward Zulu as the massive black African started away from the guard station carrying two AKMs and a ring of keys.

They encountered another set of double doors, almost identical to the first.

Track swung both AKMs forward. "Ready," he snapped.

Zulu twisted the key in the lock and wrenched the door handle down; the right-hand door swung open.

"I surrender," a terrified voice called in Russian.

Track edged forward through the doorway.

A solitary uniformed guard stood beside a chair, his hands raised, his knees shaking.

Track walked up to the man, the muzzles of both AKMs nearly touching the guard's abdomen.

In Russian, Track snarled, "Open all the cells! Release all the prisoners."

"Yes—yes, Comrade."

"I'm not your comrade. Now, move!"

Zulu quickly frisked the guard before the man picked up his keys from the desk top and walked unsteadily to the far wall.

The keys would activate a set of massive bars that automatically locked or unlocked all the cells at once.

Track heard the upper locking mechanism move. Already Track was slipping out of his backpack. Unzipping the top flap and reaching inside, he pulled out a plastic explosive with two concealed detonators in each, one obvious, one impossible to find without shredding the material.

He activated the primary detonator and wedged the plastique against a structural wall at the corner. Then he left the charge, joining Zulu as the second locking bar was activated and the cell doors sprang open.

As Track pointed the AKMs at the guard, Zulu left to set his charges.

Faces—haggard, worn, fearful—peered from some of the open cells.

Track announced, "We have come to free you and to destroy this place. There are weapons near the dead guards beyond those doors, if you can use one. Any of you who have difficulty walking will be helped. We have a means of escape. Everything will be all right."

He wished he was really that confident.

"Ready!" Zulu shouted.

"You cannot just leave me—" the uniformed guard pleaded.

Track looked at the man. "No, I can't leave you. But one false move and I'll kill you instantly. Help with the injured—be quick about it."

He had come a long way, Dan Track reflected, but he would never go that far. There was a difference, an important difference, between killing because it was needed and murder.

Track shoved the man along, looking back as the human misery began to file from the cells. There were nine men and two women, their bodies emaciated, weary looking beyond belief. Most of them sported welts and bruises on their arms and necks and legs, as well as the row of marks of electrodes.

One very skinny, very old man could hardly walk, and Zulu went to him, speaking to him a moment, then raising the man up and placing him gently over his shoulder.

Track had to force himself not to turn away from the figures he saw. If there had ever been a question in his mind of the validity of what he had spent the last several months doing, the question was resolved. In the faces of the freed prisoners, amid the care and the tears of some, the eyes shone bright.

He shook his head to clear away the thoughts. Then Track glanced at his watch. "Let's go," he murmured to Zulu. The black man only nodded. The charges would detonate in seven minutes.

GEORGE STOOD, STARING. "Why are you looking at me like that?"

The man was emaciated. There were bruises on his body. His hair was very gray, and he squinted in the light that streamed through the open cell door.

"You wouldn't recognize me," George said, shaking his head.

"I've been shuffled back and forth from one prison to another for more than twenty years," the man said. "How do you expect me to recognize anyone?"

"Twenty-six," George corrected him.

"About that. What year is it?" the man asked.

"It's 1985."

"Ha!" the man exclaimed. "Yeah, about that. I had a wife. Beautiful girl. She was pregnant. I wonder if—"

"She had a son," George whispered, barely able to speak.

"I guess I can tell you that the Russians got everything else out of me with drugs. If this is some kind of trick, I don't think there's anything left to tell they don't know. I worked for the CIA. I never could tell my wife. Never could tell anyone. My wife had a kid brother, hell of a kid—wild, but smart, you know? I think her brother hated my guts—"

"His name is Dan," George said.

"Yeah. How the hell—"

"Your wife's name was Diane. She was beautiful."

"Was?" the man looked confused, upset.

"She died a few months ago. A man who pretended to be you was responsible for her death. But he's dead now."

"You knew Diane? Did the baby—"

"The baby grew up."

"Was it a boy? We wanted a boy. But then when I started working for the CIA, well, I couldn't tell her, you know, and I think she started to—" And the man started to weep. "I think she thought maybe I didn't love her anymore."

"No, she didn't think that," George whispered.

"It was a boy, then. Is he—"

"He's fine."

"What's his name?"

"George Wilson Beegh."

"How . . . how you know all this, mister?"

George dropped to his knees beside the bunk, folding his arms about the frail shoulders, his hands drawing the head against his chest. He was crying.

Behind him, Chesterton called, "George—got to hurry!"

The man George embraced whispered, "George?"

George said a word he had never said with feeling in his life. "Dad!" And he held the man very tightly because there was nothing else in that instant he was capable of doing.

5

She had changed in the bathroom of the hangar, the woolen skirt replaced by woolen slacks, a heavy, hooded mink parka over her sweater. Her gloved hands held an Uzi submachine gun. Beside the pilot, Hideo, she watched the lights of Norway fade, the darkness of the sea beneath them.

She heard his voice coming through her earphones. "You worry, Miss Desiree."

It was a statement, not a question. She said nothing for a moment, then, "You've got the plan down pat, Hideo?"

"Yes, Miss Desiree. I fly just above the ground to avoid radar. If we are identified, I push this button—" he gestured to the recorded-message cassette in the tape recorder mounted near the radio. "The message is garbled, in Russian and with heavy static. Response to the disorder at Beria prison. Priority flight for the KGB—like that." And Hideo laughed. "And then I cross my fingers, close my eyes and keep flying."

Desiree said nothing.

"After I have penetrated Soviet territory, I land in a farmer's field the Jewish underground will have marked with flares. I wait on the ground four minutes and in that time, a truck should enter the field and stop at the far end. The truck will proceed to the helicopter, and five men and one woman of the team and three political prisoners will board. Once they are aboard, we go airborne and the truck detonates two minutes later. We fly low toward the sea and use the next tape.''

''And the next tape contains?''

''Another message in Russian, garbled and with plenty of static.'' Hideo looked at her and grinned again. ''The tape says that the raiders who attacked Beria prison are fleeing along the Neva river toward the Gulf of Finland and this aircraft is in pursuit and requests all other police and military helicopters to join in the pursuit by the time it passes the cruiser *Aurora*.''

''Are you familiar with the story of the *Aurora*?'' Desiree asked impulsively.

''No, Miss Desiree.''

''It fired a single blank round to signal the start of the 1917 Bolshevik revolution.''

''I can fire missiles at her,'' Hideo volunteered.

''No, Hideo. One leaves even an enemy their culture. What do you do after the other helicopters join?''

''I activate the third tape,'' the Japanese mercenary pilot answered. ''The third tape requests one of the trailing ships to join me cutting over the city to cross Krestovsky island to head off the terrorist powerboat as it leaves Malaya Neva and enters the Gulf of Finland. Once we have crossed over the maritime park of victory, I turn north for Finland, flying straight up the gulf after using my missiles to disable or down the accompanying helicopter. Simple. And then when we land in Finland, you give me an extra twenty-five thousand plus the second half of the original twenty-five, and I drop you at a small rural airfield. I leave by private car for Helsinki and you guys leave for wherever.''

There was no harm in telling him—but there was no sense to it, either. They would cross over Sweden and land in Norway, then fly by business jet to Heathrow airport near London, where they would refuel, then without disembarking fly on to Mexico City, refueling there before going to Acapulco.

She was weary considering it. But there would be time to rest soon enough. Before the final phase was begun. And she would help Dan Track in this as she had helped him over the months in Russian. And then once this last phase was over, there would be time again—forever, she hoped. So far his identity had remained secret, and perhaps they could live a normal life in his country or hers. Perhaps.

Desiree Goth stared down at the water beneath— nothing but darkness. Blackness.

She could barely hear the rotor noise over the sounds from the radio headset she wore, and she was warm in the mink parka. But sleep was nothing she could afford now. Desiree Goth sat up straighter, adjusting her seat belt, gripping her Uzi submachine gun.

She would not sleep again until Dan Track was beside her.

COLONEL DMITRI JURGENOV took the Czech CZ-75 from his holster and worked the slide, chambering the top round. He looked at his subordinate. "What progress at Beria prison?"

"There have been explosions, Comrade Colonel."

"Excellent—they are ready to move then. Just excellent. They are doing just as I expected." Jurgenov laughed, finding his *chopka* and settling it on his head, then grabbing his coat. It was a warm coat and he shrugged into it, edging the flap holster for the 9mm Czech auto forward over his appendix.

He took a last sip of his coffee and set the cup on the wooden table, turning toward Lieutenant Nevotny. Jurgenov let himself smile. "They have finally done just as I wished, Nevotny. Finally. I was this close to them." Jurgenov held up his thumb and first finger a quarter of an inch apart, then laughed as he started to pull on his woolen glove liners. "This close the last time. But they did not do as I expected. But I knew they would reach out for Beria prison. I just knew it. And they did not disappoint me. That is why I know it is the American, Track." He pulled the leather gloves on, then walked past Nevotny toward the door of the frame building at the far edge of the small airfield on Gutuyevsky island. He placed his hand on the doorknob. "You see, Nevotny, it must be this man Track and his comrades. They alone precipitated the defeat at the institute near Alma Ata. The KGB does not believe me. They insist it is an American counterintelligence team. Or perhaps a British unit hired by the Americans. But I have known all along. That is why we waited here."

"But our orders, Comrade Colonel—"

"One learns that orders can sometimes be damned, Nevotny. I was told to position my personnel on Dekabristov island, as you are well aware. But what if I had? Surely Track and the others would have realized that I lay in wait for them and altered their plans accordingly. But here, far away from Beria prison, they cannot know that I wait for them. That I anticipated them. My orders were predicated on their attacking the submarine base, but I knew they would not. I outsmarted them, and now we will get them."

"But the orders, Comrade Colonel."

Jurgenov sighed loudly as he looked at the unimaginative Nevotny. "There will be an official reprimand, and then a commendation. One will cancel out the other. And I will have killed this American Track and that insolent boy who is still with him." Jurgenov wrenched down on the door handle and stepped out into the cold.

A driving snow unleashed its fury against his face. But he walked ahead undaunted toward the waiting car. While all was in confusion, while panic reigned as forces were hurriedly moved toward Beria prison, he would close in.

Jurgenov clapped his hands together, pulling his chin down toward the high turtleneck collar of his white sweater.

"I will be victorious." He laughed as his driver opened the sedan's door and he started inside. "Victorious." In the distance across the field, the helicopters were waiting.

6

The first of the explosions had gone off, ripping away the roof of the scientific laboratory. As Track moved to the window again and watched, flames licked hungrily skyward into the night. Snow fell in the prison yard below, and the snow was flecked with orange in the firelight.

Track looked away from the window. Under Tatiana's direction, Baslovitch and Zulu were gathering and photographing scientific documents.

"Hurry it up, guys," Track snapped, glancing at his watch.

"I'm through here," Tatiana volunteered.

"Everything we need," Baslovitch said, as he pulled his mask back into position.

Track turned his face away from the window frame, his ears ringing. Then a second explosion rocked the night. "That's George and Sir Abner at the prison complex. Let's get the hell out of here," Track ordered. Then he and Tatiana shrugged out of their backpacks, and from the sacks they extracted four rapelling ropes, with grappling hooks on the ends.

Track affixed one of the grappling hooks, Tatiana another, Baslovitch the third and Zulu the fourth.

Baslovitch climbed over the windowsill, knocking free a few remaining shards of glass and slate of windowpane, settling onto the ledge outside the window.

Zulu followed him, taking the first rope and starting down. Track helped Tatiana swing a leg over the sill, then boosted her out to Baslovitch, the former KGB major helping the woman to the climbing rope. She started rappelling down, with Baslovitch almost directly beside her but slightly lower.

Track took the last rope in hand, looked back into the room and then began to descend the wall.

He looked down and across the prison yard, where a truck was starting to move—a big Ural that looked like a GI deuce and a half. The coffin maker had told them the truck would be waiting for them.

Uniformed guards were attacking the van they had arrived in, and then the vehicle exploded in an orange oil-and-gas fireball. The booby trap Tatiana had set had gone off. Track looked down to see her as she touched the ground beside Baslovitch and Zulu.

Track pushed off and dropped the remaining fifteen feet, landing in a crouch. Zulu had already crossed the yard toward the advancing truck, his submachine gun cutting down two KGB technicians coming toward him with pistols blazing.

As Baslovitch ran from the wall with Tatiana beside him, their subguns at the ready, Track took his lighter from his utility-belt pouch and rolled the striking wheel under his gloved thumb.

Men were rappelling down after them from the window above, and Track lit the rope he had descended, then the other three. The fast-burning fuse intertwined through each rope sputtered and burned quickly.

With the fire racing up the wall, Track ran into the yard. The truck with George and Sir Abner aboard slowed as Baslovitch and Zulu climbed into the rear cargo bed and Tatiana slid into the passenger seat.

Track looked behind him and up the wall. A uniformed KGB guard was on each of the rappelling ropes, starting awkwardly to climb back up as the fuses burned beneath them.

But they would be too late. Track looked away as the first explosion from the specially modified strip of plastique braided into the center of each rope erupted, followed by three more, shredding flesh and bone as the men were blown from the wall.

When Track reached the moving truck, fire was burning everywhere through the prison and research unit. "Go for it," Track shouted, and the truck picked up speed.

Track looked into the truck bed. A few men and women were huddled together, the intended victims of the Soviet chemical and biological experiments. He saw the face of the dissident, antiwar Soviet poet, one of the three political prisoners held at Beria. He saw the face of the Soviet biologist who had attempted abortively to share knowledge of Soviet antipersonnel biological research with the world press. Then his gaze settled on the third prisoner, whose identity had been unknown beyond his nationality—American. Track stared hard at the man. "Robert?" he asked incredulously.

The man looked in his direction, staring with vacant eyes.

Track tore down the mask covering his face. "Robert?" he repeated.

"Dan?" the man asked tentatively.

George knelt beside the emaciated, obviously tortured man there in the truck bed. "It's my goddamn father, Dan."

Track wanted to go to the man, a man who had come back from the dead. But there was gunfire, and he heard Zulu responding with his submachine gun.

Track drew the mask back up over his face, then in three crouching steps was at the back of the truck, swinging the MPK forward, seeking a target. There was more reason than ever to escape now.

With gunfire from the prison walls raining down on them, Track leveled his subgun toward its major concentration and fired repeated bursts of 9mm hail. Over the roar of the gunfire he heard George yell, "Dan, Sir Abner's crashing the gate!"

Track braced himself at the rear of the truck. Zulu was on his left, Baslovitch on his right. On impact, the truck seemed to hesitate, then stall a moment before racing ahead, the engine whining.

Track fired the MPK, and let it fall to his side on its sling. Snatching a grenade from his utility belt, he shouted to Zulu, Baslovitch and George to do the same.

When all four of the men had grenades ready and the pins pulled, Track shouted, "Now!" and four fragmentation grenades hurtled through the air toward the gates, shredding the guards who were firing from concealed positions there. Chunks of the gate soared skyward, and spear-sized slats of wood rained down, impaling the dead and the dying.

As the truck swayed dangerously around a curve, Track glanced at his watch. They were on schedule and on course. He was waiting for something to go wrong.

7

"There! Follow those lights!" Jurgenov commanded. As his pilot banked into a turn, Jurgenov heard the background radio chatter drone meaninglessly on. His six silent helicopters were closing in, he knew.

He had picked the possible sites where a low-flying helicopter would whisk Track and his team away from his grasp. Dmitri Jurgenov had followed the pattern of the raids and had concluded that Leningrad had been carefully chosen as an attack site—it was the nearest major Soviet city to an escape route. And the only escape would be by air.

The pilot's voice came to him over the headphones but he did not listen. He felt someone tapping at his arm and he turned to look at the man. The voice came through his headset again, "Comrade Colonel, we are being ordered to assist the KGB. A truck has been spotted heading for the Neva, and it is suspected that there is a boat waiting for them. A helicopter has apparently spotted the boat, but the helicopter is experiencing radio difficulties."

"They would not use a boat—they will fly from there," Jurgenov gestured toward the spot of ground where a moment earlier he had seen lights. "We will stand back and wait."

"But if we remain in hover, Comrade Colonel, without running lights, without any sound to betray our position, in this snow and darkness any low-flying aircraft could crash into us."

"You will obey orders!"

Jurgenov heard the pilot instructing the five other gunships of the squadron.

He never moved his gaze now, staring only at the now-lightless spot on the earth below. It was one of the five sites he had selected as a landing spot for Track's escape helicopter. And the light he had seen for an instant—a stray flashlight, a headlight beam—had confirmed his hunch. This was the place. He could feel it. There was an empathy, he knew, between himself and Dan Track, the only man who had defeated him in battle in his entire career. Jurgenov had studied the attacks Track and his team of commandos had made, studied the man's use of tactics, divined the man's ultimate strategy.

Jurgenov knew his enemy, and because of this he would defeat his enemy, this time forever.

He waited, hearing the pleas of the KGB coming over his radio set. He heard the orders of his commanding general in the special forces, ordering him to take up the pursuit of the truck. He would not.

THE BIG URAL CAREERED AROUND the corner into an alley, then picked up speed. Track was standing in the back, holding on to one of the uprights for support. The truck slowed again, then turned, and Track smelled gasoline and old rubber in the total darkness. He heard another truck driving past in the darkness, and the sound of brakes squeaking; then he heard a massive door closing.

Track clutched his SPAS-12 as the truck he rode slowed and stopped.

Then he squinted against a sudden light, and he heard the familiar voice of the coffin maker. "Major, you have made it!"

As Track looked into the light, he saw the Resistance fighter grinning broadly and walking toward the truck, an Uzi submachine gun slung under his right arm.

Track jumped down from the rear of the truck. Shifting the SPAS, he took the coffin maker's outstretched hand. He pulled down his face mask with his other hand. "So far so good," he said with a slight grin.

"I have spotters on the roof. The Soviets were on the trail of the second truck almost instantly, almost before it left the garage of my gentile friend here," and he laughed, clapping the shoulder of the man who walked up to stand beside him. The second man's face was a study in nervousness.

"Jews are used to this chasing around, to this fighting. It is new to me—" the man forced a laugh "—but I suppose I will get used to it!"

Track shook the second man's outstretched hand, then said, "We should start changing trucks, shouldn't we?"

The coffin maker nodded, and others came into

the circle of light surrounding the truck, clambering into the rear of the vehicle to help those inside.

Baslovitch, Zulu and George were down already, and a woman was going among Track's team doling out fresh MPK magazines from a large basket carried under her arm.

A little girl was doing the same, with a basket of P-5 magazines.

The woman stopped before Track. She had the strong build of an athlete, and her face showed a pleasant smile.

Track grinned at her, taking the magazines for his subgun, thanking her. With the pouches on his utility belt filled and a fresh magazine in the well, he let the Walther subgun fall to his side on its sling. The little girl came next, and Track handed her the two empties from his belt and the partially spent magazine in the P-5 itself before taking one magazine from the basket and putting it into the well of the pistol. Then he took two spares. The little girl's English was almost funny. "Is there a single thing the hero American would like?"

"Only a smile, darling," he told her, and she leaned up and Track bent his face toward her, and the little girl planted a kiss on his cheek.

"You have become quite the hero in my country," the coffin maker laughed. "The school children talk of you, the workers in the factories whisper of you. The women when they shop exchange hushed news of the latest raid of the Vindicators. We shall miss you and the others, Major."

"You still call this your country?"

"Yes, it is my country. That is why I do not take my family—what remains of it—and cross the border. I could. Others could. But there are Jews and Christians alike here who feel as I feel. Someday, not in my lifetime I suspect, but someday there will be freedom here.

"I'll pray you're right," Track said.

"Ready, Dan." Track turned toward Chesterton's clipped voice. Chesterton stood beside a large tanker truck at its approximate center, then stopped, disappeared beneath it and climbed inside.

"The smell should really be great," Track said to the coffin maker as they walked toward the tanker.

"It was either gasoline or milk—I thought you might prefer the milk."

"Wise choice," Track said with a laugh.

He stopped beside the tanker, hearing noises from inside it. All the prisoners and all his team were inside.

"I doubt I will have the opportunity later to say goodbye, Major," the coffin maker said. "When we reach the airfield we will transfer the other prisoners to a separate truck as we have arranged," the man extended his right hand, and said, "the people of the Soviet Union who thirst for freedom from oppression are forever in your debt. I doubt the KGB will ever recover completely from being assaulted in their strongest and most secure positions."

"We tried," Track told the coffin maker as he took his hand. And then Track ducked and started climbing up into the tanker.

The hatch beneath him was sealed, and there was a

bang on the side of the tanker and then motion. They were on their way. Track took his Trapper Scorpion and Metalife Custom L-Frame from the weapons cache that Zulu was distributing in the glow of a small battery-powered lamp. By turns, George, Baslovitch and Chesterton received their weapons, and Zulu took out a Browning Hi-Power for himself.

Track could hear George talking to his father. If they made it out alive there would be time to question Robert. Why was he considered one of the three most valuable prisoners in the Soviet Union and held at Beria prison?

But for now, Track would not rob George of even an instant of his father's company. Twenty-six years was a lifetime to recapture.

Track focused his mind elsewhere. Very soon, he would see Desiree. He doubted she had done as he told her and stayed behind in Norway. Desiree Goth was not the kind of woman who took well to orders, not at all. . . .

HIDEO WAS WHISTLING "I've Been Working on the Railroad" for the fortieth time. Desiree had considered it an odd selection for a mercenary helicopter pilot but didn't comment. He stopped whistling to say, "We're getting something strange over the radio—it is in English." He switched Desiree into the system.

English meant the Russian special forces. The reason that they used English for their communications was something she could not guess, but it was unnerving, as if they were in constant readiness for something and needed the practice.

"You are ordered, Major Jurgenov!" a voice said sternly over the static.

"I am carrying out my own plan, Comrade General. It will succeed," an assured voice replied.

"You will turn your helicopter to the pursuit of the speedboat, now!"

"I will not."

"Then you may consider yourself under arrest," the first voice said with finality, before continuing in a different tone. "This is to the pilots of Colonel Jurgenov's helicopters. You are ordered to join the pursuit of the speedboat. Lieutenant Nevotny shall assume command from Colonel Jurgenov."

"He will not! I order my gunships to remain in position!" Jurgenov shouted.

"Any pilot who obeys the orders of Colonel Jurgenov will be faced with charges. Break off now!" the general commanded.

Desiree Goth waited, listening, her hands folded in her lap over her Uzi. The *Aurora* was coming up beneath them. In the snow the cruiser looked very beautiful, she thought.

She heard Jurgenov again. "My five other gunships may join this idiotic pursuit, Comrade General, but I do not!"

"When you land, Colonel, your career will have ceased. Headquarters out."

She looked inquiringly at Hideo. His voice cut in through her headset on the com link, "Where the hell you think that cockamamie colonel is, Miss Desiree?"

"Somehow I think we'll see him, Hideo. It's time for the next taped message."

She stared at the beauty of the snow-bathed *Aurora* as the message was fed into the radio instructing one of the pursuit helicopters to break off and intercept the boat as it left the Malaya Neva.

Hideo started their machine banking to starboard. The snow had been perfect, making a speedboat traveling in darkness without lights all but impossible to spot. But there was no speedboat to search for, and if their luck held, no one would know until it was too late. She hoped.

8

Dan Track had found that by lying as flat as possible in the base of the tanker compartment he had the least chance of being smashed from side to side as the tanker progressed toward the helicopter rendezvous. There were sirens heard intermittently, but the red light bulb on which all eyes were focused, which was mounted in the very front of the tanker, had not gone on. So far so good, he thought.

He stared at the light, getting a sick feeling in his stomach as the tanker slipped on the snow-slick road surface over which they traveled, then feeling the wash of relief as the lurching stopped.

If all went well and they escaped from the Soviet Union, then the final phase of the plan—Mexico—would begin. He had almost forgotten what warmth and sunshine were like after the many months spent in Russia.

He had not missed Christmas. The coffin maker and some of his underground allies, Jew and Christians alike, had prepared a dinner for Track, Chesterton, Zulu and George. Baslovitch and Tatiana had entered into the spirit, as well. Somehow the coffin maker's sister had found a turkey and fixed it with the customary trimmings. Track would remember that Christmas dinner all his life—however long or short it would prove to be.

And he would remember the small town outside Orenburg. It had not been a planned raid, but the resistance contact had told them of the arrest of a young woman. She had been charged with anti-Soviet activity. In reality she had refused the attentions of a KGB lieutenant.

Track and his team had attacked the KGB post, freed the woman and sent her to safety through the underground. But as they had shot their way out of the KGB compound, a crowd had formed in the streets. An old woman had started to cry. An old man had started to applaud. And the street had filled with cheers as they had made their escape. He would remember that, too, Track knew. Forever.

Suddenly, the red light flashed on and Track sat up, careful that his weapons did not clang against the sides of the tanker.

Zulu was up and into a crouch. Track glanced behind to where George held his father with his left arm, and held a silenced P-5 in his right hand. If the green light beside the red light flashed, all would be safe, a road block gotten through. If the second red light flashed...Track did not want to consider it. Inside the tanker they would have no chance. They would be shot like fish in a barrel.

Track found himself smiling. Did anyone shoot fish in a barrel? He hoped he wouldn't find out.

The truck stopped.

Track looked at the faces in the red light. There was fear in the faces of the victims they had rescued from the KGB tormenters. Tatiana's blue eyes were wide as she stared toward the red light. Baslovitch's jaw was set, a P-7 in his right fist. Rivulets of sweat formed across Zulu's forehead, and his dark brown eyes were fixed, staring at the light, the Browning High-Power in his right fist.

Sir Abner Chesterton squatted, a look of calm across his face, his submachine gun across his lap. An unlit cigarette was in his mouth.

Dan Track turned his face to George. George knelt beside his father, the .45 in one fist, the Smith 469 in the other, ready. His eyes were set, his face more determined than Track had ever seen it.

Then, as suddenly as it had stopped, the truck started into motion, and suddenly all the faces were cast with green light.

One of the women prisoners made the sign of the cross. The man beside Sergei Baslovitch wept in happiness.

Track closed his eyes, and suddenly he realized he had been gripping the .45 in his fist so tightly that his circulation was going and the tips of his fingers were as cold as ice.

He opened his eyes, rolling back his cuff to study the face of his wristwatch in the green light. Taking into account the two minutes the truck had been stopped, they were a minute behind schedule.

From the increased motion of the tank trailer, he could tell that the resistance driver who piloted the rig toward the farmer's field and the rendezvous with the helicopter was thinking the same thing.

Track braced himself again in the bottom of the tanker, watching the light.

9

Daniel Hunter Track, Major, U.S. Army, Retired, stepped from the hatch opening in the base of the tanker, an Aimpoint sighted Randall .45 in his right fist, a Walther submachine gun in his left.

Cold, and the smell of fresh, chilly air made him momentarily light-headed.

He looked into the face of the driver of the truck through the swirling light flakes of snow. The man nodded.

Track spoke urgently through the escape hatch. "Get everybody out—the other truck's out here." And he stepped away, watching the second truck, a semi, closing in on them, lights out, barely visible in the driving snow.

At the far side of the field he saw lights as flares were struck. The white of the snow became tinted with yellow and orange and red, and the swirling snow mingled with the smoke of the flares. Above, he could hear rotor noises from an unseen helicopter.

It would be the helicopter Desiree had sent—he hoped.

One by one, the victims were offloaded into the night. One of the women grabbed Track's hand as Track let the subgun fall to his side, kissing his gloved hand and telling him in Russian that she would pray for him even after death. And then she walked off into the snow and the resistance people bundled her aboard the tractor-trailer.

Through the swirling snow, Track could see the coffin maker as he climbed aboard the truck cab beside the driver. The coffin maker shot him a salute, and Track shifted the .45 to his left hand and returned the gesture, then ducked beneath the tanker once again and climbed inside. The hatch sealed beneath him as he settled back onto his haunches, waiting for the movement to start again. Around him were the five members of his team, and the three political prisoners, George's father among them. Including himself, there were nine lives, he thought. The truck started ahead again, and Track braced himself for the jolting journey over the uneven field.

Track checked his watch—perfect timing.

The truck slowed, then stopped.

Track could hear the roto noise again, much louder now. He heard the slamming of the truck cab door and the rattling sounds as the hatch in the base of the tanker was opened and the cool freshness of the winter air flooded the tanker.

He let George past him, then helped Robert Beegh to the hatch. The two men stared at each other. "I think you must have hated me because of your sister," Beegh said.

"I think you're right," Track replied, smiling.

"They told me that to tell Diane would put her life in jeopardy."

"CIA?"

"Yes. But they never came for me, never tried to get me out."

Track took Robert Beegh's right hand in his. "If we make it out of here, well, it'll be good to have a brother-in-law again. And for him to have a father," he added motioning toward George.

Robert Beegh nodded, then slipped down through the hatch opening.

Baslovitch went next, Tatiana following him. Then Sir Abner Chesterton, giving Track a thumbs-up signal.

Track looked at Zulu. "You first, Major," the big black said.

"Wait a second. You know how I've always told you to stop calling me Major?"

"Yes, Major?"

"You can call me Major whenever you want, Zulu."

"Thank you, Dan," said Zulu as he crept back to allow Track to pass through the hatch. Zulu followed him.

Track could see the helicopter in the orange light of the flares, but the flares were being extinguished now by resistance workers.

As Track started toward the helicopter, light flickered from the far side of the field, then from behind him. Track wheeling toward them, his submachine gun in his left hand. "You are surrounded, Major Track. You will now die!" a voice boomed.

"That asshole Jurgenov," George shouted.

Track brought the Aimpoint-sighted Randall .45 quickly to eye level, putting the red dot over the cen-

ter of the three lights from the edge of the field, and
fired. The light out. Shifting the .45 to the right, he
put the red dot over another light and squeezed the
trigger. Another light exploded into darkness. Behind him, submachine gun fire ripped—but it was
too near to be enemy fire. Track shot out the third
light and he shouted at the top of his lungs, "Get to
the chopper! Hurry!"

As Track started to run, there was gunfire everywhere, and the sounds of running men shouting battle cries and curses from the perimeter of the field.
The resistance fighters abandoned the flares and
fired into the night. Track cursed under his breath,
firing toward a phalanx of men appearing from the
shadows. Tatiana and Baslovitch were near him now,
and he saw Tatiana grasp her left thigh and go down.
Baslovitch's subgun erupted with fire.

From the helicopter, Track heard a voice. Desiree!
"Hurry—it is only the Colonel and one compliment
of men! Hurry!"

Track wheeled toward the voice, and started to
run. Tatiana's right arm was across his shoulders, her
left arm across Baslovitch. There was gunfire from
overhead now, and the snow around Track's feet
plowed up. Over the gunfire he heard George shout,
"I'm hit!"

As they reached the helicopter, Track threw Tatiana aboard. He saw Desiree's face at the fuselage
doorway. Track grabbed her and kissed her hard on
the mouth. "Get airborne and get that chopper overhead," he ordered. "Then come back for us if we're
still alive." He ran as Desiree called after him. Track

fought to ignore her words—there was something still unfinished.

He glanced back to see Desiree helping Robert Beegh inside, then the poet and the scientist.

George should have gotten aboard but Track had known he wouldn't.

Zulu was locked in an automatic weapons duel with two Russian special forces troopers, and Track ran toward him, spraying his subgun at the Russians. One of them went down, then the second as Zulu fired again.

Desiree's chopper was airborne, and the snow was beaten into a blizzardlike frenzy. As the chopper lifted high overhead and the snow resumed its normal pattern, he saw Baslovitch swatting a man down with the butt of his subgun, then shooting him in the head. Chesterton was firing an AKM with each hand.

Then Track saw the face he had been looking for, the one he had seen in battle those many months back near Alma Ata. And he saw George, his left arm loose and limp at his side, his subgun blazing, cutting down the men nearest Jurgenov. "George!" Track yelled. But his nephew kept going.

GEORGE BEEGH RAN, his wounded leg burning, his left arm numb at his side. But he, too, had recognized the voice and seen the face. He killed two of the Russian soldiers before subgunning Jurgenov across the thighs, the special forces colonel falling to the snow.

George fell beside the man, their faces inches from

each other, blood and spit flecked on Jurgenov's lips. "What—what—"

"You asshole," George hissed, hauling himself to one knee, his left leg outstretched and screaming with the pain. But George ignored it. The death of his mother, the things that had been done, horrible things, in his father's name, the ultimate lie of the man who had impersonated Robert Beegh.

Jurgenov somehow represented it all to him—the senseless cruelty, the minds that allowed such tyranny to exist.

He turned the Russian over onto his stomach, and Jurgenov screamed with pain.

There was an explosion overhead, and he realized it was one of the two helicopters, but he didn't know which. Fiery debris rained down to the field as he shouted to Jurgenov, ramming the muzzle of the sub-gun against Jurgenov's rectum. "Asshole—huh!" And George pulled the trigger and Jurgenov's body seemed to slit up the backbone. There was an instant's scream and then there was total silence.

Except for the beat of the helicopter rotor blades.

Then he heard Desiree's voice over a megaphone. "There will be more coming—hurry! Hurry!"

George started to his feet, but the left leg would not work at all now.

As he looked up he saw Track beside him. "Feel better?" Track asked, gesturing with his subgun toward Jurgenov.

"No," George replied. "I thought I would."

"I didn't think you would," Track continued. "Come on, I'll help you to the chopper."

"Was that murder?"

He watched his uncle's eyes in the firelight of the burning debris. "Yeah, it was. I don't know what else to tell you."

George shook his head, and let himself be led by Track.

When they reached the helicopter, Zulu pulled George up into his arms and handed him aboard to Chesterton and Baslovitch. George kept his eyes on his uncle as Dan Track climbed aboard.

Desiree yelled, "Get us out of here, Hideo."

"Right, Miss Desiree," came the reply.

George felt the lurching sensation of the chopper lifting off, and he watched as Baslovitch assumed the co-pilot's position. Desiree attended to his left arm, while Tatiana looked after his leg. He looked at his father, and his father's eyes bored into him. His father had seen what he had done. Sir Abner Chesterton crouched beside him. "George, pretty soon we'll be out of this horrible place. In a few days we'll be soaking up the sunshine in Acapulco. I was down there once for the Consortium, you know." Chesterton smiled, taking George's cigarettes from beneath the black tunic, then lighting one for him, exhaling the smoke in a long stream and placing the cigarette between George's lips. "Lovely place— you'll like it. Those señoritas—tanned, dark hair, long legs. You'll love it—take my word on that, dear boy. And in a beautiful climate like that, those wounds of yours will heal very quickly. You'll be your old self in no time."

Chesterton stopped talking as George, looking at

him, inhaled the cigarette. Then George looked away from Chesterton to Track and Zulu.

They had positioned themselves by the open fuselage doorway, had donned flak vests, and were locking a heavy machine gun into its cradle.

Baslovitch was shouting over the rotor noise, "I'm getting something over the radio. They've used flares and discovered they were chasing nothing along the Malaya Neva. They are unable to get into contact with the helicopter our pilot friend shot down. Wonder why, hmm?" George looked at Tatiana as she worked on his leg, and she smiled at him. For the first time, George noticed the bandage on her left thigh where part of the trouser leg had been cut away. Baslovitch was still talking. "The dumb bastards finally deduced that the mysterious KGB helicopter with radio troubles and lots of static is really the escape craft—five points for them."

"I'd say a gold star might well be in order," Chesterton said with a good-natured laugh.

Then George heard the Japanese pilot's voice. "We're over the gulf now. I'm flying so low I'm getting spray on the windshield up here. Keep your fingers crossed, guys! If I'd known Miss Desiree was hiring me to extract you guys, I tell you I would have done it for free!"

"I'll take that deal, Hideo," Desiree Goth called back, laughing.

"Forget I said that," the Japanese man added quickly.

George said to Chesterton, "Help me to the other

door. We can get that open and you and I can use the subguns from that side, just in case.''

"You feel up to it, George?"

"Hell, yes," George said with a weak smile.

Chesterton thought for a moment, then shook his head and said, "Stout fellow—to the fuselage door we go then!"

George propped himself up as the door opened under Chesterton's hands. He dumped the magazine from his subgun and replaced it with a fresh one. Desiree handed George a second subgun, and for the first time he noticed that she carried one of her own, an Uzi.

Her black hair was windblown, and her blue eyes sparkled as she crouched beside him, tugging up the hood of her parka. "It's cold here. How are you feeling, George?"

"I'm fine."

"Good; I'll be here with you."

"All right. Good for you and Dan to be together again?" he asked.

She smiled. "I'll say." She hugged his arm for a moment. "And it's good to be with you again, too, George." George looked away from her to the whitecaps perhaps six feet beneath the helicopter, and he stared into the darkness, waiting for the lights he knew would appear. Helicopters. He clutched the Walther MPK subgun, waiting. Desiree was talking to him.

"After we take care of this last phase in Acapulco," she said, "we can all take a good long rest. Perhaps we can go to Nice. It's lovely there, and you'd love the French girls along the beaches." She laughed, holding his arm tighter. "I'm happy for you, I really am. Finding your father alive after you thought he had been murdered. I really am so happy for you."

"Stop trying to make me feel good," George snapped finally.

"What do you mean, George?"

"The Russian colonel—all right? I mean, he did things to me, and I swore I'd get him. He was already wounded, helpless, maybe dying, and I rammed this up his ass—" he gestured with the subgun "—and I pulled the damn trigger. Dan wouldn't have done something like that, would he—would he?"

She didn't release the hold on his arm. "No, I don't think so, George. But you and Dan, however much alike you are, well, you're different, too."

"Yeah." George nodded.

"Do you want my advice?"

"Yeah—maybe. Depends."

She laughed a little, putting her head against his cheek for an instant, George feeling the softness of the fur mingled with the softness of her hair. "All right," she said, cocking her head back, the hood of the parka falling, her hair cascading over it as it was caught in the wind. She was very close to him. "You and Dan both fell into this. Neither one of you was determined to be the policeman for the world. Dan was teaching SWAT procedures, survival tactics, weapons use, writing books and articles, consulting—things like that. He had a comfortable life doing what he enjoyed. You hadn't even determined what you wanted to do—"

"When I grew up," George added with a laugh.

"I didn't mean it that way," Desiree continued. "You had just gotten out of the Air Force and taken that job as a nuclear courier. You never had a chance to decide in which direction your life would go. But you are young. When we finish in Acapulco, there will be time to get to know your father. Time to get to know yourself. To find a girl you want to share everything with—like I found a man to share everything with in Dan. And maybe you can put all the killing behind you, maybe you can start over, George."

He saw lights across the whitecaps, and he wondered if in some secret part of himself he had hoped they would come. He told Desiree Goth, "Well, I can't start over yet, can I?" He gestured toward the incoming helicopters.

Baslovitch's voice rang back from the cockpit, "Here they come!"

10

Track had unloaded the SPAS-12, replacing the double O buck rounds with slug loads for possible use against the helicopters if they got close enough. But the SPAS was across his back now, and in his hands was one of the Steyr-Mannlicher SSG countersniper rifles Desiree had supplied, the Mannlicher 3x9 variable scope still attached. Crouched beside Zulu and the 7.62mm PKMS machine gun mounted before the huge Oxford-educated African, Track worked the levers for the scope mounts, rotating them to unlock, then sliding the scope and rings and mounts off the receiver of the .308 in one fluid motion. He handed the scope to Tatiana, shouldered the rifle and looked over the iron sights toward the helicopter lights approaching from port. ''In another ten minutes we'll be in Finnish air space,'' he heard Hideo call back.

Track didn't answer. Ten minutes could prove an eternity. In the darkness, he waited.

The helicopters were closing in quickly. Baslovitch called back, ''I'm getting a radio message in English—must be special forces—telling us to turn back toward Soviet territory.''

''Stall them as long as you can with the radio-static thing, Sergei,'' Track shouted.

"Doing just that, and they don't like it. We are ordered to head for Soviet territory or be shot down."

"Well, son of a gun," Track said with a laugh. "Tell them to fuck off then."

"Roger on that message—will comply," Baslovitch shouted back.

Track settled the sights of the SSG on the running light of an approaching chopper. The armor-piercing .308s would penetrate the bubble and either disable the craft or the man flying it.

Track worked the bolt, chambering the first round from the five-shot rotary magazine. Steadying the rifle, he adjusted his position. The front sight fell into the notch, and Track worked the rear set trigger. His finger brushed lightly against the forward trigger and the rifle discharged, rocking against his shoulder.

The helicopter he had drawn a bead on veered to port suddenly, falling back, skimming downward nearer the water surface.

Machine-gun fire opened up from the other pursuit craft around them, and bullets whizzed through the fuselage. Track shouted, "Everybody down if you're not shooting back! Cover your heads!" He speedcocked the bolt, settling on the same chopper again, firing.

The chopper seemed to hesitate, and then a brilliant fireball consumed it. The noise of the explosion was deafening, and as it faded, Track could hear the others in the helicopter cheering. "Owe it all to clean living," Track said as he speedcocked the bolt, searching for another target. Beside him, the heavy machine gun had opened up under Zulu's hands. The helicopter banked slightly, and Track knew the Japanese pilot had fired a missile.

A helicopter almost directly aft of them exploded, and huge chunks of burning debris fell into the sea.

Track settled on his new target, working the set trigger, then touching the first trigger; a running light shattered out.

Another missile fired, but this one came toward them, the contrail gleaming white against the black surface of the sea. Zulu swung the machine gun toward it and fired, and the missile exploded in midair less than a hundred yards from them.

There was no time for the set trigger. Track had the bolt cocked and snapped through the first trigger, sending a bullet toward the control bubble of an approaching chopper. He worked the bolt again and fired the last round. The machine that was his target veered away and out of sight.

Another helicopter was closing fast, and Track handed off the Steyr-Mannlicher rifle and swung the SPAS forward. The machine was very close now, its guns blazing. Track started firing the SPAS into the doorway beside him while Zulu fired the machine gun. Their helicopter took more hits, and Hideo shouted, "We can't take much more of this!"

"Sure we can," Track shouted back as he fired. The enemy helicopter exploded in midair, and Track felt a heat wave race across his skin.

From behind him, he could hear the rattle of submachine guns as George and Chesterton fired from their doorway.

Hideo fired another missile, and another enemy ship went out of control and crashed into the black water below.

A contrail started toward them, and as it got closer and closer, Hideo lurched the gunship violently upward and into a steep portside bank. Track nearly fell from the fuselage door as the contrail crossed beneath them and the missile tore into one of the Soviet gunships that had been on their starboard side. With the tail rotor gone and the tail section of the fuselage afire, the ship crashed down into the sea.

The gunship leveled off, then down, as Zulu fired again. Using an AKM now, Track fired toward one of the pursuit craft. As Zulu's and his fire concentrated, the craft suddenly lurched violently, nosing down into the waves and was gone, the water surface suddenly glowing bright, and then the light extinguished.

Their gunship rotated a full one hundred eighty degrees, and the forward missiles were fired, a Soviet gunship exploding in midair in reply.

The gunship climbed, then dropped sickeningly, another missile firing. Track fired a second AKM, the machine rattling beside him, the missile exploding, the gunship afire but limping away.

The gunships fell back now, and over the roto noise, Hideo yelled, "All right, Finland, I love ya!"

Desiree was suddenly beside Track, clutching his arms, shouting in his ear, "When I hire a pilot, I hire a pilot."

Track set down the AKM and turned on his knees toward her, then took her into his arms.

Finland. Then Norway. Then London and on to Mexico City. Finally, Acapulco. But there would be time—after all the months without her, he would make the time.

11

The prospectus from Eisenstein Petrochemicals was most interesting. A seventy-five-percent growth rate in stock values over the last two years was complemented by large amounts being spent for research and development. The contract for the experimental fuel development they had been given by the defense department was not in the prospectus.

He tossed the prospectus to his desk and started across the huge conference room, looking upward toward the vaulted ceiling for a moment, drawing inspiration from the cleanness of line, the form that followed function. It was bomb proof.

He crossed the dais and took the three green carpeted steps down to the main level, watching the faces about the gleaming chrome-and-glass conference table as they watched him.

He looked away from the faces of the men there as he walked easily toward the head of the table. He stopped then, staring at the massive mural that dominated the far wall. A map of the world done in ceramic tile, measuring fifty feet from end to end, some twenty feet from top to bottom.

It was not big enough.

Without looking at the men at the conference

, he began to speak, his hands thrust deep into pockets of his slacks. "When I took over the torate as Master, the organization had not em- d upon a major undertaking since the so-called oil embargo."

nd he wheeled toward the faces at the conference le. "Years—years of inactivity!"

He hammered his right fist down onto the glass, hen raised himself to his full height, running a hand through his hair to push it from his face. "The organization was moldering, gentlemen. The most powerful organization in the history of the entire world was moldering." His voice had adopted the tone of a parent explaining a difficult concept to tiny children. "The Directorate has power that has been unused, and I pledged to correct that. Our current undertaking is the first step."

A hand was raised timidly, and the Master looked at Oliver Sprackton, his blue pin-striped three-piece suit immaculately tailored, his white shirt gleaming, his solid dark blue tie knotted in a perfect Windsor. His balding head gleamed under the lighting that was suspended over the table.

"Yes, Oliver?"

Sprackton stood up and began to speak. "When you became the Master, profits were up, our control over various corporations was expanding at a satisfactory rate and all was prosperous. I saw no need to change a policy that had remained in effect since the last Master assumed control of the Directorate at the close of World War II. I mean no criticism at all but, if we assume a more aggressive posture, as has been discussed, that will mean being saddled with a higher profile. And for centuries—''

The Master interrupted him. ''For centuries, there have been rumors that we exist. And if we ceased to exist at this very moment, the rumors would persist. It is part of the public consciousness to see manipulation behind world events. You forget, Oliver—'' he lit a cigar with the gold table lighter, flipping the lighter in his hand as he paused ''—that without the leadership of my grandfather, World War II would never have started. And the financial benefits we reaped would never have come to us. It was unfortunate that he died in 1945, and more unfortunate still that the man who replaced my grandfather as Master chose to follow such a conservative path. There were many golden opportunities for us—the Korean War could have been escalated. The recession that followed could have been deepened, turned into a full-scale economic depression like the one that all our families so greatly profited from in the 1920s and 1930s. And then as a gesture, he became involved with the Arab oil embargo. How clever of him. The Vietnam conflict could have been expanded and all the rubber-producing interests could have been ours. We could have taken over the Japanese electronics industry easily, very easily—but no. No, Oliver—and all of you—inactivity, resting on the profits of our past achievements is absurd.

''Since Oliver has brought this up—'' the Master intended that he bring it up, feeding him the lines that he had known would provoke the mild outburst ''—we should address the larger issue.'' He left the cigar to burn in the ashtray, standing up, beginning to circumnavigate the glass-and-chrome conference table along the green carpet as he spoke, watching which faces turned toward him, noting who looked away, whose eyes were alight with his personal energy, who showed revulsion. "For centuries, we have worked behind the scenes. At different times various groups were blamed for what we did, and during the Middle Ages some secret society was invented in the popular mythology, but no one has ever dreamed that such a society, vastly more powerful, vastly more secret, really existed at all."

He clutched his hands together behind him now, much like an admiral pacing the deck of his ship. "It is not impossible to assume the world would be a much different place without our leadership today. But leadership that is lateral only cannot be fully exercised. Just as the character of the Directorate and its composition have changed drastically to keep pace with the times, such a change is once again demanded." He stopped walking, raising his voice for a moment. "*Demanded*, gentlemen." He continued his walk.

"It is time that the Directorate exercised its power to best advantage under an organized program." And the Master allowed himself a smile. "We shall come out of the closet, as it were, gentlemen—reveal ourselves."

Oliver Sprackton sat down.

The Master had once more reached the head of the conference table, and he continued his oration.

"We will achieve a monumental first step in this

direction at the completion of the Eisenstein acquisition.'' He pressed one of the buttons on the console at the head of the conference table and turned to face the ceramic map. A video screen was sliding into position as a rectangular section of the map slid away, disappearing into the wall surface. As the video screen became flush with the ceramic map, mariachi music began to fill the room and the screen showed an aerial view of Acapulco, Mexico.

A narrator's voice began, ''Welcome to sunny Mexico's sunniest spot—exciting Acapulco!''

The lights in the conference room gradually dimmed as the image in the video screen grew more well defined, more intense, and the Master sat down in his chair, making a tent of his hands to cover his eyes. After the ten-minute promotional tape about Acapulco, there would be a fifteen-minute film assembled by Eisenstein Petrochemicals that had been made for the defense department and that revealed some interesting data regarding the nuclear irradiated rocket fuel that Eisenstein scientists claimed would double the output of conventional rocket and missile engines while using the same volume and weight of fuel. Following that, a five-minute videotape, culled from news broadcasts, would show Eisenstein's specially built supertanker.

And then to more mundane things—the mechanics of how and when and by what means the Directorate would acquire Eisenstein Petrochemicals, topple the Mexican government, irreparably damage United States government credibility in Latin America and destroy every living thing in and around sunny Acapulco.

The Master enjoyed listening to the mariachi music as he scribbled the note in his agenda, using his personal shorthand that only he and one other person could read: "Oliver Sprackton's eldest son, Morton. Better choice for Directorate board. Arrange that Oliver be permanently replaced. In lieu of flowers, make donation to heart fund."

He closed his agenda and continued to listen to the mariachi music.

12

Dan Track hadn't thought it would be possible—and he wondered if it was a sign of growing old. He stared at the ceiling. They had touched down in Finland, then flown by private jet to Norway where Desiree had rented a house. The doctor aboard the plane had treated George's wounds, then begun examining the three freed inmates of Beria prison—malnutrition, the effects of beatings, but apparently nothing that time and care would not heal.

At the house near Koppera along Norway's border with Sweden, they had eaten a modest but warm meal, perhaps consumed more liquor than prudent and then Dan Track and Desiree had gone to bed. He remembered stripping away his clothes and lying across the bed while Desiree had talked to him from the bathroom. He remembered hearing the sound of her brushing her teeth.

And then he remembered waking up.

Desiree was not in bed beside him, and her place was no longer warm. He looked at his watch; it was nearly one o'clock.

He pushed the covers down and swung his feet out of the bed and stood up.

The door to the room opened slowly, and Track instinctively reached for the Trapper Scorpion on the nightstand.

But it was Desiree. "I'd just come up to wake you," she said with a smile. And he noticed her gaze was fixed slightly below his abdomen.

He looked down at himself, then grinned. "Combination of just getting up in the morning and thinking of you." There wasn't any robe and he had no desire to scrounge any of the clothes he had shed the previous night.

He walked into the bathroom, talking to her as he did what he had to do. "When do we leave for Heathrow? I'm still a little fuzzy."

"Not until around five o'clock. I arranged it that way because I assumed everyone might want to sleep in a bit."

He flushed the toilet and looked at his face in the bathroom mirror. He could see Desiree's reflection as she stood in the bathroom doorway. Her hair was up, teasing downward from the nape of her neck. She wore a heavy-looking pink quilted bathrobe, and her hands were stuffed into its pockets. He prepared to shave, plugging in the electric shaver, telling her, "I'm sorry about last night. All I could think about every night when I'd go to sleep all those months—well, you know. Last thing I expected to do was conk out on you."

He almost dropped the razor. Her hands had tugged at the belt of the robe and she shrugged her shoulders. He still stared at her reflection. The robe fell away and she was naked. "I thought I'd give you a second chance, Dan."

Track set down the razor and turned away from the mirror to face her, suddenly more aware of his own nakedness than he had been when he had gotten out of bed.

He walked toward her, folding his arms around her waist and drawing her close against him, feeling her nipples hardening against him. His hand found her breast, kneading it, and his mouth crushed her slightly parted lips.

He moved her closer to him, feeling her hands as she touched his back, his chest, then his crotch.

He swept her up in his arms, carrying her to the bed. He dropped on one knee to the mattress, setting her in the warm spot he had just vacated, then slid in beside her. She drew the sheet and the down comforter up over them as Track's arm curled around her, his fingers entwined in her hair, gently pulling her head back. She was smiling and he kissed the smile. Her hands moved over his chest, then along his back as he slipped between her thighs, the heat there burning into him. He could feel her hands against his rear end, and he kissed her lips, her neck, her throat, her breasts.

She pushed him back, rolling him over, and her lips brushed at his cheek and then at his chest, her fingers knotting in the hair there, her mouth drifting down along his abdomen.

And then he felt her mouth on him and his back arched and he looked down along the length of his body, her eyes raising to look at him. And the pressure of what she did eased a moment and she spoke. "I love you—forever."

Her body moved over his, her legs straddling him, and suddenly he was inside her, his hands caressing her hard nipples, her head cocked back, then forward, her hair cascading around them both as she moved a pin from its place.

His arm encircled her neck, drawing her mouth down to his. Her body moved and Track could think only of this woman. Her body was shuddering and after a very long time, after rolling over together and Desiree moving beneath him, his body shuddered as well, as if it would never stop.

ON THE FLIGHT TO HEATHROW, Desiree had slept in the chair beside him, her head against his shoulder. Zulu and Sir Abner Chesterton had played chess. Sergei Baslovitch and Tatiana had played backgammon and talked. George and his father had just talked. The other two freed prisoners—the scientist and the poet—had slept, as well.

Through arrangements Desiree had made with Sir Abner Chesterton's British SIS contacts, the two Russians were being taken to England for political asylum.

At Heathrow, the plane had refueled and flown on, Zulu and Chesterton played another game of chess, Robert Beegh slept in his chair, and George stared out the cabin window by his seat, saying nothing. Track sat opposite Desiree at a small table in the forward portion of the private jet, Desiree smoking a cigarette, Track nursing a double shot of Seagrams Seven with ice and a splash. As if he had asked her, Desiree began to detail the arrangements once they arrived in Acapulco. "I've rented a house along the beach. I would have bought it—a marvelous price—but that wouldn't have fitted in with the plan, so I just rented it. It's under the name Jack Dustinowski Associates, as you had asked—that's an odd name."

"It's been a CIA front company for years," Track replied. "JDA manufactures and distributes exotic industrial explosives."

"All right. And I worked out all the details with your friend from Chicago—"

"Rafe Minor."

"Yes. He should already be at the house. I had him flown from Chicago to Paris, and in Paris he picked up the false passport and the other materials identifying him as R. L. Cunningham. Through some of Sir Abner's contacts in SIS and some of my contacts with the Mossad, we invented a background linking R. L. Cunningham to the CIA as a contract agent for the past nine years. The hardest part was getting your friend Miles Jefferson to cooperate—"

Track interrupted her, laughing. "Well, I never said Miles was my friend, exactly," he said.

"Well, it's the Honorable Miles Jefferson now, member of the United States House of Representatives."

"Then he won in November. How's his leg?"

"He limps and uses a rather stylish-looking cane, but he seems fit. He wasn't very eager to go along with this."

"I didn't think he would be, but if anybody could sell him on it, you could."

"I also spoke with your friend Mr. Capezzi. It

turned out that he and I had done business together several years ago and we'd met socially before that—"

"Crazy Carlo Capezzi isn't my friend, but he made an offer to help me once and I'm taking him up on it, that's all. From everything I understand about him, despite the position he's held in the Cosa Nostra, he's a man of his word."

Desiree smiled. "Mr. Capezzi actually seemed overjoyed to repay his debt to you. But he also said that the debt would never be fully repaid, that you should feel free to call upon him at any time for a service. He was exceptionally pleased to learn that he would not only be aiding you, but helping his country. He put at our disposal a man he considered to be among his very best."

"What about planting the seed?" Track asked her, finishing his drink and getting up and walking to the small bar and pouring another.

She was beside him suddenly, taking down a glass that she filled with an ounce of Cutty Sark and a splash of water. "I've hired a man named, well, his name isn't that important—"

Track looked at her. "You don't trust me?"

"Yes, of course I trust you. His name is Axel Staudenmeier, a West German. What a ridiculous thing to say." She looked away. Track bent and kissed her forehead. Desiree looked up at him and smiled. "Anyway, Axel is an information broker. I've used his services a few times. I don't really like him—he plays both sides of the street, as you might put it."

"He's a double?"

"He feeds information to the East Germans and to the Americans. But I got information to him indirectly that the CIA was meeting all of us in Acapulco, and a member of the U.S. government was going to be there to confirm the offer of political asylum to the defecting Soviet KGB major and his girlfriend. I indicated that the CIA contract agent in charge of the operation was R. L. Cunningham and that a team of contract employees would be working with Cunningham to provide security while the representative of the U.S. government—Miles Jefferson—sat in on the preliminary debriefing to make certain Baslovitch wasn't a plant being sent in to feed the government false information. I also said that Baslovitch didn't trust the Americans, and that was why the whole thing was going down in Mexico."

"You did good, kid," Track said with a smile, sipping at his drink.

"You really think this is going to work?" Desiree asked.

"Sergei knows that the top American agent is somebody named Potempkin—runs the whole KGB show for the United States, Canada and Mexico." Track started back to the table, sitting down. As Desiree sat down opposite him he watched her. She wasn't looking at him, but apparently plucking some imaginary piece of lint from the full skirt of her navy-blue dress. She was apprehensive about something. He guillotined a cigar, lighting it in the blue-yellow flame of his battered lighter. She looked up at him from across the table and smiled.

"This Potempkin," Track continued, "keeps a

low profile. Nobody, except the guys who actually run the KGB, knows his identity. But Baslovitch got to know Potempkin's number two, a woman code-named Hummingbird. Baslovitch says he doesn't really know what she looks like. The three times he met her her appearance was totally different. Once she was using the cover of a hooker. Another time, she was a young high-school girl. The third time, she looked like an old lady.''

Desiree shook her head.

"What's the matter?"

"It made me think of my brother, Krieger—the disguises."

Track reached across the table to her, squeezing her hand beneath his. "We both need to get away from this."

She nodded, not looking at him. "What else do we know about this Hummingbird?"

"Nothing, really, except that Hummingbird would have to know how to reach Potempkin. And Hummingbird would be sent in to Acapulco to supervise KGB attempts to kill Sergei before he can talk to Miles and this R. L. Cunningham we invented. When Hummingbird makes her move, we make ours and put the bag on her."

"How will you get her to talk?"

"Sergei's got the stuff that should do the trick. If she's had drug-resistant training against interrogation and Sergei's stuff doesn't get the information out of her, well, we'll think of something else."

"I don't like this," Desiree almost whispered.

"There's no other way to get at Potempkin. If we

can nail Potempkin we can disrupt Russia's entire North American network. It could take them months to even begin to reorganize. And with the information we can get from Hummingbird and hopefully from Potempkin himself, we might be able to give the CIA, SIS, the Mossad—all the free-world intelligence agencies—enough of a strategic advantage that the Russians would never fully recover. Just imagine for a minute what Potempkin must know."

Desiree started to light another cigarette, and Track reached across the table and lit it for her. She exhaled a long thin stream of smoke as she spoke. "What if Hummingbird outsmarts you, Dan?"

"Then we could all wind up dead," he told her matter-of-factly.

13

Harlen Mills had never done anything like this before, and he was at once mildly excited and yet full of trepidation.

In the sixties, he had been a member of the SDS and had never crossed over formally into the Weathermen. But his sympathies had always been with them. Through a girl he had slept with, he had been able to feed data to various campus radical organizations—the girl had been a police stenographer. Eventually he and the girl had married and then divorced. But during the marriage, he had joined the Communist Party.

There had never been much to do, except go to meetings and talk about the day the revolution would come, and go into neighborhoods where nobody knew you and pass out leaflets and sometimes get punched in the face for the trouble.

There had never been much to do until the fall of 1980 when he had been introduced to the girl with the very long brown hair who looked as if she still might belong in high school. She had let him make love to her, and afterward she had told him that the name he had been told wasn't her real name at all; her real name wasn't something he should know, but he should call her "Hummingbird."

Harlen Mills sat behind the wheel of the rented Volvo in the Acapulco parking lot, thinking about her. That she used him was clear, and he'd liked it. He had become a courier for her. He had run a safe house for one of her agents; the agent had been a homosexual and this had been unsettling to Harlen, made him question his own sexuality. But then Hummingbird had relieved both his body and his mind and he had been happy again.

Harlen Mills looked at his face in the rearview mirror. He was forty-one, but didn't quite look it. His red hair was thinning, but not badly. There was a thread poking up beside his neck on the left side where the button-down collar of his shirt was slightly fraying.

He looked away from the mirror, startled as the door of the Volvo opened.

He knew it was Hummingbird even though the hair color, the eye color and the clothes were wrong. But like everything she wore, they were right for her. "Admiring our pretty face, are we, Harlen?"

"No," he said, at once not liking it yet liking it when she teased him as she always did.

"Sunny Mexico—I haven't been here for a while," she said with a soft voice.

He looked at her, taking in the auburn hair, the green eyes, the elegance of her expensive sandals, slacks and blouse, all the same shade of pale gray. "I got the car just like you said. I drove past the beach house you told me about, and I left the message with the hotel clerk you told me to see. My suitcase is in the trunk; don't you have any luggage?"

She smiled and raised the massive cloth purse from the seat between them. "Just this and this." She nodded toward the maroon stuff bag across her lap. "I always travel light, Harlen. Did you learn the map of the city like I suggested?"

"Yes," he told her.

"Good—here's a test question, then." She rattled off an address. "Do you know it?"

"I think I can find it."

"Good—we have some friends to meet there and then you and I can hop into bed, if you like."

Harlen Mills cleared his throat. "Do you, ahh, do you really like me?"

She looked at him and she laughed for an instant, and then her face lost the laughter but her eyes shone brightly; that could have been the effect of the contact lenses, he supposed. "As a matter of fact, I really do," she said, and leaned across the seat and kissed him once lightly on the lips as he stared at her. "Goes to show how dumb I am, but I really do."

He closed his eyes for a moment. She could have been lying. He told himself she wasn't. He turned the key and started the engine, shifted into first and eased away from the parking space. He could hear her opening the glove compartment. "You brought two guns," she said.

"The hotel desk clerk gave me the package, and I opened it as you told me to."

"Do you know anything about guns, Harlen?"

He looked at her as he strained second and shifted into third, blending in with traffic, the sun blindingly bright. "No, except that I don't like them."

"Do you want to carry a gun?"

"No. I don't know how to use one."

"I'll just leave the second gun in the glove compartment, then." He heard mechanical noises, suggesting to him that she was seeing if the gun was loaded. He glanced toward her again—it was a black, ugly-looking gun, and it disappeared into her huge bag. "I was elaborating on your accomplishments to Potempkin. And I told him I liked you, too. He sounded impressed."

"That you like me?"

He heard her laugh as he downshifted into second, but then got his break in traffic and was able to upshift instead. "No, not because I like you. But with the work you've done for the party and the work you've done for us. He said if there were more people like you, the cause of world communism would be further along than it is." And she laughed again. "Those were his very words, Harlen. You should be proud. I'll bet they'll even hear about you in Moscow, Harlen."

"Fat chance of that." He smiled, trying to picture the city map in his mind so he wouldn't get terribly lost. He'd always been good at memorizing things and done exceedingly well in school. He managed a fast-food restaurant now and had always felt quite consciously that life had cheated him.

"Maybe after we get this traitor we're after and his friends, well, maybe we can take a trip to Moscow together. Would you like that, Harlen?"

"I'm using up my last ten days of vacation now."

"We wouldn't have to wait until next year. You

could always lie and say that you were sick and getting specialized treatment in Moscow." She laughed again.

"I'd like to go to Moscow, see how it really is. I get so sick of people in the United States. Everybody after their damn profits—"

"You don't have to proselytize to me, Harlen. I'm a Communist, too."

He made a fast right, doing a quick change from first into third as he finished the turn in order to impress her. But he had to slow, dropping into first because an old man was walking in the street pulling a red coaster wagon behind him. When there was a break in traffic he took it, passing the old man and his wagon and climbing back up into third.

"You might not like Moscow as much as you think, Harlen. Remember, you're used to being in the United States and speaking out against it and for communism. Things are different back home."

He looked at her—he was sure he was on the right street now. "Do you miss Moscow?" he asked.

"It was never home to me—I was born in Minsk. I probably shouldn't say this," she said as she lit a cigarette with the dashboard lighter, "but I don't think I could ever go back permanently, unless I lived someplace near the Black Sea. I like a little wilder life than you can have in Moscow. Well, you know that." He heard her laugh again as he looked away to pay attention to his driving.

"I think I love you," he told her. He didn't even know why he had said it.

"I think you do, too," she answered, and he

looked into her eyes. He had no idea what she really looked like, except for her body. He had made love to her as a brunette, as a blonde, as a redhead, and auburn haired as she was now. He'd never put much stock in the theory about natural blondes, advanced in the novels by Mickey Spillane. And he didn't like American novels anyway—the heroes were always impossibly heroic and impossibly right wing. He was waiting for her to say something else, and he purposely missed his next turn so they wouldn't reach the safe house and she would have the excuse to change the subject. The silence was long and then finally she whispered, "Do you want me to say I love you?"

"Yes, but only if it isn't a lie."

"I love you. You missed your last turn, Harlen—we have a schedule to keep."

He just looked at her and he nodded.

He made the next right, then a quick right after that. "If you know the city, why am I driving?"

"Because you don't like it when I drive."

"You drive too fast."

"You drive too slowly—did you ever think maybe that's it?"

"I don't know."

"But I do love you, Harlen. And that's really silly, isn't it?"

He didn't look at her.

"You aren't the best lover I've had—I don't say that to hurt you. And you aren't the most handsome man I've known. You're a good lover. And you're good to look at. And you are smart, Harlen—but not the smartest man I've ever met. But you're a nice person and I value that more highly. So I love you."

"But as Potempkin's number two, you'd—" he didn't want to finish the words, let alone the thought.

"Kill you or sacrifice you? Uh-huh. You say you love me. I can't change being me because of that. So, yes, but I don't think that will ever happen. If it worries you, we can be late for the appointment." He stopped the car in front of the Spanish architecture ranch house partially visible beyond a high wrought-iron fence and large green hedge.

Harlen Mills shut off the key. He told himself that if he had a soul, he had just given it away. He looked at her. Her hands came to his face, her mouth touching lightly against his, then harder, harder than he thought a woman could kiss a man. His hands closed on her body, kneading her flesh beneath the silk blouse.

Their lips parted and he held her close to him, feeling her hands holding him. "It'd be nice if we could both fly out of here," he whispered.

"Nice doesn't count much, does it?"

"No, it doesn't count much."

"I may have to sleep with Peter Scorese. He's very insecure ever since the problems he had in Atlanta that I told you about. But I don't like sleeping with him."

"Don't talk about it."

"I wanted you to know, that's all."

"What if they're watching from the house?" Harlen asked Hummingbird.

"They can report me to Potempkin, but he'll understand. He always does."

"Can I meet Potempkin someday?"

"You've already met Potempkin and never realized it. We're trusted—that's the important thing."

"No, this is the important thing." He kissed her hard on the mouth again and felt her hands moving in his hair, her nails touching at his scalp and his whole body starting to disintegrate.

And then she stopped and her hands pressed against his chest. He opened his eyes.

"Take me into the house—and remember, Harlen, as far as they're concerned you've been on this kind of operation before and it's none of their business when. They'll think you're my lover, and that's all right this time."

"All right."

She straightened her clothes as she sat back and he asked her, "What's the real color of your eyes?"

"Green—the contact lenses just make them greener."

"Your hair?"

"Brown, but not as much red as it has in it now."

"What's your real name? I don't mean the whole thing, just your first name."

"If you knew my real name, you'd be killed."

"By you?"

"Maybe, so I won't tell you." She opened the door and stepped outside.

He watched her across the seat for a moment. Then he reached into the glove compartment and took out the second gun. It was ugly and black just like the one he'd seen her put in her purse. He held it in his right hand. She stooped down and looked at him across the seat. "It's an M-K P-7 9mm semiautomatic, Harlen. Why? In case I try to kill you?"

"No. I don't know why."

"Take the extra magazine for it. And the chamber should be loaded, so don't pull the trigger."

"I wasn't planning to." He put the gun in the inside breast pocket of his blue blazer. It made the coat sag as he got out of the car into the sun.

She had the maroon bag over one shoulder, the purse suspended from the other. "Bring your suitcase, Harlen."

"All right," he said as he locked the driver's side door and heard her door slam. He went around to the trunk and took out his case, and then turned and followed her toward the house. She stopped at the gate and rang the bell. She looked at him and she smiled.

14

The sun was setting as he rode his horse northward along the beach, the splash of the surf all but drowning the splashing of the animal's hooves. On the horse beside him rode Thomas Beal. He looked at the man and asked, "Why did you feel it was necessary for us to meet like this, Beal?"

Beal's eyes were dark, cold and gray, deeply set into his well-tanned, heavily creased face. "Well, it's not often the generals come out into the field, and we field commanders always like to get in a few words about the welfare of the troops—shit like that."

The Master nodded, laughing. "But I'm only here for a vacation, one last vacation in one of my favorite places. By the time the operation takes place, I'll be long gone. So I'm not here as a general, only as a tourist."

"But you're still the general."

"And you're still the subordinate, then."

"That's right, I'm the guy that gets paid to risk his life, to put the old family jewels in the wringer if anything goes wrong."

"Nothing will go wrong—it never does," the Master told him. He thought of himself that way. A name was like any other name, but the Master had true meaning. And he was the Master. "Was there something specific or were you merely interested in ruining my afternoon ride?" He slowed the horse, reining in, the animal shifting under him as a breaker crashed around its legs.

"Well, the idea of ruining your afternoon ride sounded good, that's true. But I wanted to talk to you about the word that came down from your little executive assistant."

"Desmond?"

"Yeah, old Dessy. He sounded awful damned casual telling me to ice this fella Track and the other ones. The woman is Desiree Goth."

"I know that—rather a side benefit, actually. Her gunrunning to the antigovernment forces in—"

"Don't tell me," Beal interrupted, looking up from stroking his horse behind the left ear as the animal tossed its head.

The Master's horse jumped a little under him. "Then what's your problem," he said, "Don't want to kill a woman?"

"That has nothing to do with it. And there are two women—some Russian dame that came in with the KGB major. But this is a CIA operation now, and there's a member of Congress down here in on it."

"Who would that be?"

"Miles Jefferson. Used to be with the FBI. Got shot up in some big hush-hush operation and left the bureau and went to work in his father's law office while he ran for Congress. He won."

"Black, isn't he?"

"Yeah, he's black, but that doesn't mean shit one way or the other. I don't like getting my orders from old Desmond when it comes to maybe knocking off a congressman."

The Master laughed, watching the tip of his cigar.

"Is he *your* congressman, Colonel Beal?"

"No."

"Well, then there's nothing to worry about. I want this Major Track, Desiree Goth, the Englishman Chesterton, all of them, dead. That means Miles Jefferson and the CIA team that come down to interrogate Baslovitch—all of them."

"This Eisenstein Petrochemical deal does occupy a little of my time."

"Let us suppose," the Master began, heeling his horse ahead slowly along the surf, "that this Major Track is actually in the employ of the CIA. He and his people are probably the ones spoken of as the Vindicators."

"That's another thing," Beal commented, riding beside him, lighting a cigarette with a disposable lighter. "I kinda like what these Vindicators did inside the Soviet Union. Never been too fond of Commies, you know."

"They have their uses—in the broader picture."

"But I don't like killing a bunch of guys that were doing something I would have liked doing myself."

"Very touching, Colonel, but not very practical."

"If Track and these other ones are the Vindicators, all you've got to do is leak word to some of your

Commie friends who they are and where they are and the KGB will do the job free."

"My sources indicate the Soviets have already taken steps to pursue Major Track and the others here to Mexico. But if the KGB had such poor luck on their own territory, you'll forgive me if I'm a bit loath to trust to chance. I want Track and the others dead."

"All right, consider it done—but not until you tell me why."

The Master looked at him, laughing a little. "You realize I could have you killed at any time."

Beal let his Windbreaker fall open as he unzipped it, the breeze catching it, blowing it back, a small submachine gun in some kind of shoulder holster revealed beneath it. Beal laughed and drew together his jacket. "One picture is worth more than ten thousand words, like the Chinaman said."

"This man Track and the others may not be here by coincidence," the Master said, "and should you or any of your personnel be even slightly indiscreet or foolish and he should become privy to any information concerning us...well, it could prove awkward. We're better safe than sorry. A wise businessman, Colonel Beal, just like a wise military commander, tries to eliminate obstacles before they present themselves in his path. And you would do well to remember my instructions that we were not to meet except in the direst emergency. You have violated that principal premise of your employment. Never violate it again."

"Then why did you agree to meet me?" Beal

asked, reining in both the Master's horse and his own.

The Master stared along the beach toward the Aztec temple shapes of the Acapulco Princess hotel. He envied the man who owned it—at least for another few days. "You mean, why didn't I have you hired through an intermediary, to insulate myself in the event your tongue should someday prove loose?"

"Yeah, why?"

"Think of it this way, Colonel Beal. The Mafia has its code of silence—*omertà*, I believe they call it. Various intelligence agencies have certain ranks of employees who might well be counted on to utilize death pills of some sort to silence themselves rather than divulge secret information. In the case of our relationship, I have total faith in you. You would not talk if asked, and if forced, you would choose death."

"Why?"

"You have a large family—brothers, sisters, aunts, uncles. Your older brother owns a controlling interest in a small savings and loan. Your youngest sister likes to take her cub scout troop on field trips into Manhattan. Your father requires a particular type of medication on a daily basis in just the right dosage— too little or too much per capsule and he would die. I know—" the Master threw his cigar down into the sand as he watched Beal's gray eyes "—that you are aware of the peculiarities of fate. For were the slightest hint of suspicion to be directed toward me because of you, very suddenly fate would turn against all your loved ones. In very unpleasant ways. I never hire a man for a responsible position under the Directorate unless he has a family. Good day.'' And the Master smiled.

He didn't ride off into the sunset, but rather along the beach and parallel to it.

15

It was a classic safe house, and its security made sleeping at night a little easier, Track thought, as he stared out at the sunset over the water. There was no cover within two hundred yards of the beach house on the three landward sides, and the distance from the house to the water was another two hundred yards. For a sniper to do his thing, the sniper would have to be very good and very well equipped.

The three-car garage was enclosed and attached to the house. The owner of the house, who had rented it to Desiree through an agent, had wanted to preserve the natural beauty of the beach and of the ocean. Therefore, all the utility lines, and this included telephone, were buried deep beneath the sand and only surfaced inside the rather uncharacteristic full basement.

Because of the landscaping of the veranda, which faced the shoreward sides of the house on all three sides, a fast-moving man under fire could get from one place of concealment to another in seconds.

Dan Track smoked one of his familiar cigars as he sat with his back to a palm tree. The surf was less than a hundred yards from him. Tucked inside the waistband of his swimming trunks was a Smith &

Wesson Model 60 Chiefs, like the one Desiree usually carried in her handbag. Leaning against the palm tree was a partially closed beach umbrella, and fitted to the shaft of the umbrella were two clamps. The clamps held a mini-Uzi with a silencer fitted to it.

But the guns were not significant in his mind. He was simply relaxing, squinting at the sunset over the Pacific through the dark lenses of his sunglasses, feeling the sun's warmth on his chest, arms, legs and face.

"It's me," a voice announced from behind him.

He didn't look at George. "Okay, me—sit down if your leg bends and enjoy the sunset."

He heard a groan and then George was beside him. George rarely dressed as though he was relaxing. This afternoon was no exception, and the young man wore boot-top Levi's, track shoes, a cowboy shirt open at the front with the sleeves rolled up to just below the elbows. His Jack Daniels baseball cap was perched on his head.

Part of the bandaging was visible on George's left arm.

Track looked away, back to staring toward the sunset. "How's the leg, George?"

"It moves okay, Dan."

"So how was your dad doing?" Track flicked ashes from his cigar. "I assume that's who you were on the phone to."

"That hospital in Mexico City was a good idea. He said he's getting his appetite back a little and getting more strength in his legs."

"That hospital specializes in treating people who don't want publicity."

"Why I didn't stay in Mexico City with my dad, right?" George asked.

"Right," Dan Track answered.

"I figured I'd see this through."

"I'm glad to have you here, but I just wanted you to know that's all."

"Yeah," George muttered, and Track heard the sound of George lighting a cigarette, smelled the smoke on the air. He puffed on his cigar. "You want a beer?" George asked.

"Why—you got one?"

Track looked at his nephew, and two bottles of Carta Blanca appearing from George's left side. Track took one and twisted off the cap, setting it down beside him, "Here's looking at you." Track took a swallow. Carta Blanca wasn't his favorite beer, but it was satisfactory.

"When do you think?"

"Think what? When will Miles Jefferson arrive from the airport or when will the KGB come and kill us?"

"Either one, or both."

Track looked at his watch. "Miles should be here in a few minutes. The KGB? Search me. Hope it isn't too soon. This is kind of a nice beach house to let it get all shot up."

"After this is over, I'm gonna take some time and, ahh—"

"Yeah. I'm gonna take some time and, ahh myself," Track said with a laugh.

"Desiree?"

"Yeah. Your dad?"

"Yeah, we've got a lot to catch up on."

"I know what you mean," Track murmured softly, pulling on the beer again.

"How about after all this?"

"You mean after we nail Hummingbird and get her to lead us to Potempkin?"

"Pretty much," he heard George answer.

"Well. Sir Abner can get his old job back at the Consortium. Desiree has a business to run and Zulu's going to help her. Just like before."

"And what are you going to do? Work for the Consortium?"

"No, I don't think so. Maybe I'll settle down with Desiree, make an honest woman out of her. Zulu could run her business. I could start my own VIP protection outfit or something like that. I'm not sure." Track laughed. "Maybe I'll go into the gun-runner business with Desiree, huh?"

George didn't say anything.

Long bands of sunlight lay across the water like streaks of gold. "What are you going to do?"

"Shit—hell if I know. You know me."

"You could work for Sir Abner—the money's good."

"Yeah, the money's good, better if I could get your job. I suppose we could always work together."

"Yeah," Track said with a nod. "I guess we're going to have to play it by ear." He didn't feel up to committing himself to anything definite.

"Look . . ." George began.

"I know," Track said, regarding his nephew, then standing up. He handed George the half-finished bottle of beer. "Here, you finish it—I've got confidence in you."

"Where you going?"

"Back up to the house."

"I'm gonna sit here awhile."

Track started barefoot along the sand, but he stopped. A man on horseback was on the rise to the south, perhaps a quarter of a mile away. It wasn't the first figure on horseback he'd seen since they had moved into the house. He shrugged and kept walking.

He had left his sandals and his shirt at the edge of the red-tiled apron that fronted the house on the seaside just beyond the driveway leading down from the road. Track crossed the gravel driveway and stepped into his sandals, snatched his yellow knit shirt from the wrought-iron fence post where he'd left it and slipped it on.

He pulled the shirt over his gun as he walked inside the house. He felt sorry for Baslovitch and Tatiana— to keep up the front they were not allowed outside the house. Since they were the ones the CIA was supposed to be interested in, they were the ones under tight security, and it would have looked strange to any KGB observers if Baslovitch and his woman were careless.

He saw Zulu beside the pool, and Track angling off from his course toward the long, low, nicely landscaped terraced steps that led down from the house. Standing at poolside wiping his body down with a towel, the huge African looked even larger than usual. "Bet the water level dropped a good six feet when you climbed out."

"Ahh, Major, it is marvelous to note that life's trials and tribulations have seemingly no uplifting effect on your rather abysmal sense of humor."

"Trying to flatter me won't get you a thing," Track said with a grin as he dropped into one of the metal-framed chairs surrounding the pool. "Where's Desiree?"

"With Sir Abner. As you know, they decided to pool their personnel resources in Acapulco in order to provide some fresh intelligence. They should be returning shortly." Zulu set down the towel and picked up a white terry-cloth robe, slipping it on as he continued to speak. "For some reason, my presence was deemed more a liability than an asset. Sir Abner's theory, I believe, was that my physical presence might adversely effect the willingness of his informants to speak freely."

"It's that wonderful way you have about you, Zulu—always setting people at perfect ease."

"How gifted you are at stating the obvious, Major." Zulu walked along the pool's edge and took the chair opposite Track. A small round metal table was between them, and Track set his cigar case and his lighter on it. "I worry concerning young George, Major," Zulu continued.

"What—the way he iced that Soviet colonel?"

"That is only part of it, but a significant part certainly. He seems almost despondent. I think some great struggle flares within him and I fear that when our Soviet adversaries do indeed arrive to dispatch Major Baslovitch and the beautiful Tatiana, George may hesitate."

"That thought crossed my mind," Track murmured, his voice low.

"Finding that his father was kept alive all these years for the sole exigency of the imposter becoming uncontrollable was indeed good fortune. But such a traumatic experience can easily make one view life with a different perspective. And of course the events following the raid at Alma Ata..."

Zulu let the sentence hang. Track thought for a moment of his sister, Diane, and concluded that there was good reason to hate the Soviet regime. Zulu began to speak again. "George was crushed to the depths, then fired to the heights, all within a matter of months. And at an emotional zenith, he did something that he objectively and subjectively realized was morally wrong."

"Well, it wasn't really that morally wrong killing the Soviet colonel," Track said. "It was just the way he did it, the circumstances. He set himself up. He was being the ultimate tough guy. I think subconsciously he was living up to an untrue image of himself. And commission of the act brought him very suddenly back to reality."

Zulu began to laugh, and then so did Track. As Zulu rubbed the towel across his bald head, as if shining it, he intoned, "I can see it now, Major, the pride we'll have as we hang up our shingles—bargain-basement psychiatrists."

Track stood up. "You know, I'm almost getting to like you."

"Perhaps some time away from the fading sunlight will cure you of the malady. Curiously, the malady does not affect me; my likes and dislikes have remained unchanged."

"Fuck off," Track said with a grin, picking up his cigars and the lighter and retracing his steps toward the house.

The telephone was ringing as he mounted the steps and one of Rafe Minor's fake CIA team—a syndicate soldier owing allegiance to Crazy Carlo Capezzi—stood by the small table at the far end of the hallway, picking it up. He looked down the hallway and nodded toward Track. "It's the Englishman, for you."

"Thanks," Track said as he reached the table and took the receiver from the man's hand. The soldier's name was Rudy, and he carried a pistol Track had never seen in serious use. It was the wrong era for it. The gun was a Mauser Broomhandle, the shorter-barreled Bolo variety with hard rubber grips rather than the more normally encountered wooden ones that so resembled a broomhandle as to give the basic Mauser its sobriquet. In a bizarre way, Track held a grudging respect for Rudy and his choice of the first commercially successful military pistol firing a flat shooting round, virtually the first Magnum-type round for a handgun. A deadly and efficient pistol even if it was a museum piece by modern standards.

He spoke into the receiver. "This is Track."

"Dan—Desiree and I will be returning as quickly

as possible. One of Desiree's contacts has given us information that is most disturbing—''

"The Commies don't care that we're down here," Track interrupted. The phone was safe—bug free and with a voice scrambler attached. Unless the KGB had someone in the telephone company switching room the conversation couldn't be monitored.

"It's not that. It's not that at all. We must expect visitors and very soon. Very soon."

"Then hold off coming in and call back later. I don't want you and Desiree walking in on the middle of a firefight."

"Agreed. Be careful."

Track broke the connection and turned to Rudy. "Get Rafe up here. There's an assault due."

The Capezzi soldier only nodded, taking off in a dead run, the shoulder holster that carried the Bolo Mauser flapping at his left rib cage.

Track jogged the few steps to the open doorway. "Zulu—we're on!" he shouted.

"I'll be glad of it," the voice boomed back.

And then Dan Track thought about George. "Holy shit," he said to himself and he reached into the hall closet and grabbed one of the M-16s before throwing himself into a dead run for the beach.

HE THOUGHT ABOUT IT almost constantly—the smell, the sounds, the way the man's body had looked. The bullets from the subgun had ripped the body apart.

George lit another Winston off the nearly dead butt of the last one, then dropped the butt into the empty bottle.

He had killed enough, he had decided.

He was part of a war now. They had fought the war throughout the Soviet Union. Now they had taken the war into North America: their objective was to capture Hummingbird and get her to lead them to Potempkin. And then remove Potempkin from the scene forever.

George swallowed hard.

The phrase "a belly full of death" came to his mind and he quietly said it to himself, inhaling the cigarette smoke. His uncle could forget it, or at least force it from his mind. It was a way of life to Zulu and to Desiree Goth, as well. She sold it on the open market. Killing. But it was not a way of life to him. Not yet.

He had decided that he had no intention of letting it become one.

George took a pull on his bottle of beer, then nested the bottle in the sand beside him. He reached under his open shirt, taking the Smith & Wesson 469 minigun from inside the waistband of his Levi's. The gun's black surface was wet with his own sweat. He stared at the automatic in his hand. Thirteen rounds with the chamber loaded as it was.

Thirteen rounds.

George licked his lips. It was not the gun—this gun or any gun—it was what was inside the man who used it. George had seen Dan Track kill countless times—but never murder.

George set the gun down on the sand beside him, closing his eyes against the dying sunlight. He listened to the surf, feeling the warmth of the sun where it struck his face beneath the peak of his cap.

BEAL PULLED THE BLACK SKI MASK over his thinning hair and across his face, twisting it so the eyeholes were where they should be. He reached under his leather sport coat and snapped the MAC-10 from the specially built shoulder holster.

On the right-hand side he carried two spare magazines. In the small of his back he carried the silencer. He started over the rise of the sand dune, screwing the silencer into place as he moved.

He thought about the Master.

Beal considered the merits of killing the man, but to set himself against the Directorate would have been suicidal, he knew. For hundreds of years, perhaps longer, no one had set himself against the Directorate and lived. He didn't know when the Directorate had taken on the acronym D.E.A.T.H. The first letter he had always imagined stood for Directorate. But as to the rest, if the acronym were in truth an acronym and had meaning at all, he had no idea and did not wish to conjecture.

But whatever the meaning, Death was the appropriate term for the Directorate and its leader. The Master of Death.

Beal's face sweated under the ski toque, but he kept moving, along the ridge of sand, toward the beach house the man Track and the others were using. That it was a CIA safe house bothered him little—the CIA, for all its much-vaunted secret budget and bony fingers in the global pies, was no match for the Directorate. Perhaps the Directorate controlled the CIA, or the United States government. Perhaps it controlled virtually everything.

After the Master had hired him and sworn him to secrecy, Beal had discreetly begun some research. He had questioned the truth of what he had been told when the Master had hired him.

It had sounded too strange to be true. The Directorate was an organization of vastly wealthy, vastly powerful men, who from their own ranks selected by some process unclear to him a man they called the Master. And the Master served in his capacity for life. These men, whose wealth and power however well-known or anonymous had been in their families for centuries, ruled the world's events from behind the scenes. It had been too much for Beal to readily accept.

As he crouched beneath the ridge of a dune and gave the silencer a good-luck twist, he wondered if that had been the reason for the Master's doing what he had done. Had it been a demonstration to wipe away all disbelief?

The one thousand shares of obscure mining stock Beal had inherited from an uncle upon the man's death some twenty years before had suddenly gone from being worthless to being valued at $320 a share. That had been at the midway point of the Wall Street day. By 5:00 P.M., the shares had become valueless again. In that same day, Beal had been contacted by the United States Army and told that his commission in inactive reserve was being reactivated and he was to report for duty by 0700 the next morning. Two hours later he had received a wire that the reactivation had been cancelled. His son by a marriage that had proven useless to both parties had been stricken seriously ill with an undiagnosed illness that caused fever to rage in the body. But an hour later, the fever had subsided and the boy had been pronounced cured. One of Beal's major credit card holders had contacted him that his credit was being canceled for some reason or another and that full payment was demanded immediately. An hour later, a telephone call had come, between the calls from his broker, the Army and the hospital, that the cancellation of the credit card had been a mistake. It was then that Beal had checked the envelope in which the cancellation had come. It was postmarked the day after the incident took place.

He had abandoned all queries into the origin of D.E.A.T.H. and its Master. He knew their power. Death, financial ruin, personal tragedy. And it had made him feel greater fear than he had felt for his first jump into enemy territory, greater fear than his first illegal border crossing, greater fear than he had felt for the wife he no longer had at the hour their son had been born and he had been snowbound at an airport a hundred miles away.

It had taught him the meaning of the word fear.

If there were a reason for the acronym, perhaps that was it—death itself was what the Directorate symbolized, what the Master of D.E.A.T.H. could will.

Beal kept moving, wondering if the sweat pouring down his face beneath the ski mask was a result of the heat or a result of remembering that solitary day when his life had been irreversibly changed.

He had threatened almost jokingly to kill the Master, and almost jokingly the Master had given him the counterthreat. It was a way, Beal knew, of keeping his own sanity and self-respect. But he would never go against D.E.A.T.H.—the Master had become his master.

He heard the sound of the motorcycle and wheeled toward it. The bike jumped the ridge of sand, and Beal threw himself to the ground to avoid being struck. Three more bikes roared down, jumping over him and onto the beach, skidding across it toward the beach house.

Then came running men, and Beal pushed himself to his feet, firing a long ragged fearful burst into the confusion of humanity suddenly flooding the ridge. He cut down three men with the MAC-10, and he started to run back the way he had come along the ridge and toward the waiting—he hoped—horse he had ridden.

The sand rippled on the ridge wall to his left and he threw himself down and rolled onto his back, firing again, cutting down two more men.

He pushed himself up, running, ripping the ski mask from his face.

He cleared the ridge, clambering up to the level of the knot of palm trees where he had tied his horse.

The horse was still there, and Beal threw himself up into the saddle, tearing the rein free so violently that he ripped it in half. His heels gouged into the flanks of the bay mare. He looked back once as the horse took him from the trees and along the beach road away from the house and the men who attacked it.

There was a battle, but the identity of the attackers was unknown to him.

"Ride, dammit!" he yelled.

The Master. He would have to tell the Master. This could affect the overall plan.

He beat the MAC-10 against the animal's sides to make it go faster.

16

George heard the furious noise of the motorcycles coming, and he knew what they represented. He stared at them for a moment, not bothering to try to get up. With his left leg wounded and the resultant stiffness in his left knee, there was no sense in running.

No point.

He looked at his gun in the sand beside him and closed his eyes for a moment.

It was beginning again.

"Hell," he snarled under his breath, grabbing the Smith autoloader, stuffing it in the right hip pocket of his jeans as he rolled left, toward the beach umbrella. His hands found the shaft of the umbrella and he worked the release, the umbrella opening, his hands moving along the shaft, finding the two quick release clamps for the subgun there, opening them. George swung the muzzle of the subgun on line and fired through the canopy of the umbrella, shredding it as he tore into the first of the bikers bearing down on him. The bike spun out wildly, and the body tumbled forward over the handlebars.

George was on his feet now, throwing the shredded remnants of the beach umbrella to his side, firing the subgun in 3-round bursts, knocking out another of the bikers.

But they were coming too fast, and as they closed around him in a ragged circle their assault-rifle fire chewed into the sand. Over the din of gunfire, he heard a shout, "Hang on, George!"

It was his uncle.

George wheeled toward the voice, pumping the trigger of the subgun until the weapon was empty. Dropping it to the sand, he snatched the 469 from his hip pocket, working off the safety and firing 2-round semiauto bursts. He thought he was hit in the left arm, but there was no time to look.

Men were falling, and the circle of bikers was breaking up.

He could see Dan Track down in the sand, firing an M-16 from a prone position, but the bikers were passing his uncle now, passing Zulu, as well, who looked incongruous running barefoot along the sand wearing nothing but a terry-cloth bathrobe, and firing an M-16. The huge African threw himself down, rolling, firing, clipping one of the bikers from his machine as the bikers passed him.

"Baslovitch!" George rasped, then he shouted it, running now despite the pain in his leg. "Dan! This was a trick—to get Baslovitch!"

The pain was bringing tears into his eyes, but he ran anyway.

THE FIRST OF THE BIKERS had reached the front yard near the pool and Sergei Baslovitch crouched beside Tatiana, his arm around her shoulders. Baslovitch held a mini-Uzi in his right hand, while Tatiana gripped a Walther P-5.

Baslovitch could see Track's black friend from Chicago, Rafe Minor, and beside Minor, two of the syndicate soldiers.

"Waste the mothers!" he heard Minor shout over the gunfire, as the bikers took the front stairs.

Baslovitch shoved Tatiana down and she half screamed in protest, but Baslovitch straddled her to keep her down, the mini-Uzi in both hands now, spitting 3-shot bursts toward the doorway, over the level of the prone Rafe Minor and the two syndicate men.

One of the bikers was into the hallway as Minor and the others opened fire. Baslovitch felt that all four of them had hit the man as the bike spun out and flew over the couch.

Rudy was on his feet, the Broomhandle pistol firing unbelievably rapidly in his right hand. The helmet visor of the second biker shattered and the body snapped back and away from the machine. The bike crashed into the telephone table, and the table shattered as the machine skidded along the wall and fell over.

The roar of the bikes from the courtyard was deafening now, but Baslovitch held his fire, and no more of the attackers came up the steps and into the house.

Baslovitch looked to the floor beside him. Tatiana was struggling up. He started to say something to her, but then he heard the sounds of gunfire from the second-floor staircase and he threw himself over her, feeling something tearing at his left arm and involuntarily screaming in pain. But his body covered her body.

Baslovitch snapped the mini-Uzi toward the staircase and fired, men with Uzi submachine guns were running along the second floor and down the steps. Baslovitch grabbed Tatiana and dragged her with him toward the near wall beside the staircase. Then he saw it—a grenade, and he was powerless to stop it.

Baslovitch closed his eyes as he threw Tatiana to the floor, shouting, "Protect your eyes from it." If it was a stun grenade they should at least be able to see. And if it was fragmentation... But the explosion of the grenade answered his question, throwing him from Tatiana's body.

As he opened his eyes, he could see a fragment of wood from a piece of furniture impaling her to the floor through her left forearm.

Baslovitch shouted, "Bastards!" as he fired out the mini-Uzi. He was up, the mini-Uzi useless on its sling at his right side now, his P-7 in his right fist as he dropped to his knees beside the woman, the ends of her blond hair were tinged red with her blood. He already had the pistol squeeze cocked as he fired into the face of one of the assassins, wrenching the Uzi from the man's body, the neck snapping audibly as he tore at the sling. Kneeling beside her as more of the attackers came down the staircase, he started spraying the Uzi, spraying and praying.

THERE WAS NO TIME to wait for George. Track ran desperately toward the house. Zulu ran beside him, then outdistanced him as they both raced after the bikers.

A man with an Uzi stood in the gateway, and Track heard Zulu yell, "Major! Down!"

Track threw himself to the sand, and Zulu fired as he rolled, then fired again. Then the big African was up, running across the road toward the red-tiled patio that extended beyond the gate. Track was sprinting, firing the M-16 as a face appeared above the wall. The face exploded. The M-16 was empty.

Track threw himself into the run. He was at the open gateway now, and could hear Zulu firing out his M-16 just inside the courtyard. A man with an Uzi came at Track's face, and Track snapped the barrel of the M-16 up, batting away the subgun. Wheeling left, his right foot snapping out, and the man went down with a vicious head kick. A second man was coming to his left, and Track threw himself forward, rolling under the muzzle of the subgun as it discharged over his head. Track's forearm brushed aside the subgun, and his other fist hammered upward as he came out of the roll, crushing into the Adam's apple of the gunman. The body snapped back.

Track dropped to his knees to fetch up the Uzi, but a third man was coming. He snatched the little Chiefs from the Hip Grip on his swimming trunks and double-actioned the revolver three times into the subgunner's face.

Track wrenched the Uzi free of the dead man nearest him and got to his feet.

He fired a short 3-round burst into the nearest of the subgunners.

No spare magazines were in evidence, and he ran

ahead, armed only with the captured Uzi, not knowing how many or how few rounds remained in the magazine. There was no time to check.

Zulu was to his left, swinging the M-16 like a war club. The buttstock of the assault rifle shattered against a human head.

Track ran ahead, taking the steps in a long stride. In the corridor, he dodged one of the motorcyclists at the head of the steps, firing the Uzi into the man's chest and neck. The bike spun out, over the edge of the steps. And the question of how much ammo was left in the Uzi was answered, as well—the subgun came up empty.

Track dove over the side of the steps, coming up in a roll on the grassy area there.

He ran toward the motorcycle, and throwing down the spent Uzi, grabbed up the fallen man's M-16, wrenching the sling free of the body. A little luck was on his side, and he snatched two spare 30-round magazines from the man's belt.

Two more bikers were in the courtyard, and he saw Zulu bulldogging one of the men from his machine, almost ripping the head and neck from the torso.

Track emptied the magazine still in the liberated M-16 toward the second biker, nearly slicing an arm from the trunk, cutting the man from his machine with surgical neatness.

Track dumped the spent magazine, ramming one of the two fresh thirties into the well.

He slung the M-16 crossbody under his right arm, and wrestled the fallen bike up from the grass and straddled the machine. Gunning the engine, he started through the courtyard. The M-16 was in his fist, and he was firing three round bursts into the Uzi-armed men on foot.

He had heard an explosion from the house, followed quickly by another.

Track killed another of the Uzi armed attackers, letting the M-16 fall to his side. Wrenching the bike into a tight circle, he gunned it ahead, shouting to Zulu, "Inside the house!"

The three steps were coming, and Track hauled up on the fork, giving the machine all it had, bouncing one step, then another and then nearly going over as he reached the level of the main entrance to the house.

He sped down the corridor, the M-16 at his side.

Beyond, he could hear gunfire, see flames. Men were coming down the steps from the second floor.

Track shouted, "Look out—comin' through!"

He hauled up on the fork again, gunning the engine. Reaching up with both hands, he grabbed a chandelier and let the bike rocket ahead without him.

The Honda Gold Wing crashed down into a knot of attackers, and screams split the air as the gas tank exploded and the acrid smell of the burning gasoline drifted over the air.

Track swung from the chandelier toward the staircase, letting go as he crossed over the staircase into the attackers coming from the second floor, hurling his body into their midst.

A tangle of arms and legs resulted, and curses shrieked in Spanish and English—and Russian.

Track was falling, rolling backward down the

staircase, twisting his body. He wedged himself against the banister as men hurtled down the stairs past him. His hands found the M-16 and he swung it forward. The assault rifle on full-auto he sprayed across the stairs, killing.

Gunfire erupted from behind him. The light crack of the Bolo Mauser was followed by assault-rifle fire, and more of the attackers went down.

Suddenly the M-16 was empty in Track's hands, and no more attackers were coming down the staircase.

His hands were shaking as he slowly came to his feet, wondering if anything was broken. Everything should have been.

He heard the crackle of flames, the loud hiss of a fire extinguisher.

He could hear Baslovitch and Rafe Minor shouting orders.

His hands still trembled.

He thought of an expression the adventure novelist Josh Culhane had used when they had fought the Malina terrorists together in Las Vegas. And under his breath Dan Track murmured it now, "Let's see Sean Dodge top this." And Dan Track sat on the steps and started to laugh.

THE FIRE WAS OUT. Tatiana's arm was wounded, but she walked with Baslovitch supporting her. Bob, the other syndicate man on loan from Carlo Capezzi, had a bloody laceration across his forehead but was mobile. Rafe Minor was kicking dead men in the head to make certain they really were dead or correct the problem if they weren't.

In the doorway, George and Zulu stood together.

Rudy, a grin on his face, was reloading his Bolo Mauser.

Dan Track looked at his hands. With conscious effort he could stop them from shaking.

At least that's what he told himself.

17

"They abandoned the beach house before the police arrived. I don't know where they are," Peter Scorese told her.

Hummingbird looked at him. "You are very clumsy. All those men. All those weapons. And none of Track's people killed, one of the CIA personnel wounded. And they got away. All your men dead or left for the police. What if one of them talks?"

"There was only one Russian and he was killed. None of the others knew why the hit was called."

"You make me sick—you impotent man," she said with fury in her voice. Standing, she thrust her hands into the pockets of her pale green skirt and walked across the living room in her bare feet, trying to think. "How soon before we can find their new location?"

"I, uh, I don't know—"

Hummingbird turned toward him quickly, brushing a lock of hair back from her face. "What *do* you know?"

"Look, this wasn't—"

"Oh, no. It wasn't your idea, not at all. You are more bother than you are worth, Peter. It is as simple as that."

"But, Hummingbird, Comrade Ghermanyevitch knows I'm—"

"Incompetent! Yes, he knows that. Potempkin will be more displeased with you than you could imagine, Peter. I wouldn't want to be you at all."

"I can make it up, I can—"

"Oh, you certainly will. But you'll never redeem yourself."

"I've always been loyal to—"

"To the party," she snapped, gathering her skirt under her as she plopped down onto the sofa. She drew her legs up, arranging her skirt. "The party has plenty of people who are loyal. What the party needs, what any organization needs, is competence. How you ever survived in the CIA as long as you did is a mystery to me. If you had been that bad in the KGB, you would have been dead years ago."

"What about this Baslovitch guy?" Scorese persisted, raising his voice, walking toward the window overlooking the street. She watched him. What a stupid man, she thought. "What about Baslovitch, huh? All this time a KGB major and everything and he turns out to be a traitor."

"Isn't that the pot calling the kettle black, Peter? Baslovitch was never a traitor to the Soviet Union. He gave certain information to a friend; it led to disastrous results. And when the Committee decided he should be eliminated, only then did he take action against the Soviet. He was and still is a brave man. I wish I could say the same for you."

"I wanna talk to Potempkin."

"Oh, no you don't. Potempkin would kill you instantly. But I'm giving you another chance, a chance to find Dan Track. Do nothing but that. Find him. I'll take care of all the rest.''

"But—"

She stood up, stubbing out her cigarette in an ashtray. Then she looked across the room at him. "One more mistake, Peter, and you'll never live long enough to spend all the money we paid you over the years to betray your country. You'll just simply die, Peter."

And without looking back at him, she started across the room and toward the narrow hallway. Harlen Mills was waiting in bed for her, and her anger at Peter Scorese was no reason to upset poor, loyal Harlen. She had undressed him and he had been about to undress her when Scorese had hammered on the bedroom door. Her mind would be elsewhere now as she let Harlen make love to her body. But he would never know, because she loved him.

She opened the bedroom door and made a smile appear on her lips. "Hello, darling," Potempkin said, and closed the door.

18

It would be the last place the Russians would expect—he hoped. And after Track and his people had regrouped following the attack on the beach house, word could be leaked to entice the KGB to try again. Interrogation of the survivors of the KGB assault had netted nothing—they were Mexican contract hoodlums hired by the one Russian among the strike force, and the Russian was dead.

The weapons had been supplied.

Track sat at the telephone. No scrambler had yet been installed, but if no one knew their location—another beach house further south, this one sheltered by palms and too close to the road for comfort—there was no reason to assume the call could be monitored.

Don Carlo Capezzi came on the line at last. "Yes, Major. I appreciate the courtesy of your call, sir. How may I assist you?"

"Don Carlo, we had a bit of a problem. The Russians launched an attack against us in greater force than we had anticipated or prepared for. None of our personnel were killed or seriously injured, and that includes your associates Bob and Rudy. Michael and Alex were at the airport at the time. So all is well, but

I find myself in need of information, and I thought perhaps—''

Don Carlo Capezzi's well-modulated voice cut him off. ''You have only to ask, Major Track. Do not insult me by placing limitations of your own on my friendship toward you. What information do you need?''

''Mexican street hoodlums were sent against us, assassins one could buy for little money on the streets of any of the large cities here. The weapons they used were from the United States, M-16 rifles with U.S. government markings and Uzi submachine guns that were evidently stolen from the United States government as well.''

''You're certain of this?''

''Yeah, I am.''

''And your charming inamorata Miss Goth could shed no light on this matter?''

''She may be able to make an educated guess when she arrives here. An armory in northern California was robbed of Uzis and M-16s about nine months ago, I recall. Maybe these weapons were traded across the border for drugs.''

''I would have no personal knowledge of such a thing,'' Don Carlo told him. ''But there are some persons of my acquaintance who might be able to conduct certain inquiries. You wish to track the weapons to their source in Mexico, in order to determine who supplied these weapons to the persons sent to harm you, and then to work back from this?''

''That's my intent, if possible.''

''Give me your telephone number there.''

Track studied the dial of the telephone and read the number aloud. He had to repeat it three times, but finally, the don read it back correctly. Then, "Is there any other service you require, Major?"

"One strange thing occurred. All the weapons we used were either 9mm or 5.56mm caliber—submachine guns, pistols and M-16s. The weapons of the attackers were of the same caliber. My nephew and I each carry .45-caliber pistols, but neither of us had the opportunity to get to them. But several men were dead near the roadside. They had been killed with what appeared to be a .45-caliber submachine gun—perhaps a MAC-10. It leads me to believe that a third element is still in operation here."

"And you wish to identify this third element. Have you considered that the CIA might have gotten wind of your intentions and have agents of their own in the area, and this is why several of your attackers were killed?"

"It's possible, but I don't want to discount any other possibilities. So I was wondering—"

"You want information that will be difficult to obtain. I can initiate certain inquiries, if you like."

"Yes, very much, Don Carlo."

"A line of inquiry suggests itself to me. I'll call you as soon as there is any information. Are you personally all right?"

"A little stiff. I zigged when I should have zagged."

"And the other woman?"

"Tatiana's arm was injured. It bled a great deal but was a minor injury. She's here with us."

"Do you require any further assistance? I have many friends in Mexico."

"Not at this time, but I wouldn't object to you alerting some of your friends that they might be needed. The next move against us by the enemy force is going to tell the tale."

"Good luck to you then, my friend. I shall speak again to you soon." The line clicked dead.

Track hung up.

"Hey, Dan—Desiree and Chesterton are here."

"Right," Track said, looking up past the lighted table lamp to the hallway where Rafe Minor stood beside the opening door. He had an M-16 slung across his back and a pistol in his left hand.

Track stood up. Desiree came through the doorway first, running. Chesterton and Rudy were behind her. "When I saw the house," Desiree began, coming into his arms, "I was—" She buried her face in his chest as Track folded his arms around her. "I thought. . ." she began.

"Shh," Track whispered. "That's why I left Rudy near the house on the road. I didn't want you running into a pile of Mexican cops."

"But from the road—"

"It didn't look that bad inside. That one grenade dumped part of the roof. I was just glad you had arranged to have a second house available just in case we needed to move in a hurry."

"Rudy told me Tatiana was hurt—"

"Zulu patched her up. She's fine; Sergei is with her. Bob got a bad cut across his forehead. Sergei got nicked twice in the arm—no bones broken, though. George got a couple of flesh wounds."

"But you?"

"Well," Track said with a laugh. And he whispered in her ear, "When we make love tonight, you be on top, okay? My arms are sore, I gave my back a little twist, and my left knee has a bruise on it you wouldn't believe."

She leaned up, kissing him, then set her purse down beside the lamp and started searching through it. She didn't look at him as she talked. "Sir Abner, tell Dan what we found out."

Track looked away from her into Chesterton's eyes. The smile lines around them were gone, and the wrinkles in his face showed a weariness Track had rarely seen. "I don't know if this has any bearing on what we're involved in, but I rang up an old friend of mine who was with me in the service until he was posted here to Mexico. That was fifteen years ago. He's been head of station here for some time and has a house here in Acapulco. He told me something he said was quite hush-hush. The United States has alerted the Mexican government to put out feelers for any possible terrorist activity relating to the Eisenstein Petrochemical supertanker that will be passing about eighty miles off the Mexican coast. The tanker should be going past our area tomorrow, and it apparently contains some mysterious fuel that is highly volatile. My friend didn't like the ambiguity of the whole thing and did a little digging of his own. He learned that the shipment is several million gallons of an experimental rocket fuel. It was ferried from the east coast of the United States by water simply because it was too hazardous to transport by land, and is on its way for testing at Edwards Air Force Base in California.''

Track raised his eyebrows and looked away from Chesterton. He watched as Desiree found her cigarettes, but her hands were trembling and her lighter wasn't working. Track fished his old Zippo from the side pocket of his trousers and lit the cigarette for her.

"Get on the horn to your friend," Track began.

Chesterton was already dialing the telephone, and he turned his mouth to the receiver. "Charles? Abner Chesterton here. Yes, I've told him. I rang up to ask you another favor, old boy. Yes, one of those favors I'm afraid. Just a mo.''

Chesterton looked at Track. "What sort of gun was it?" he asked.

"Just a mo?"

"Yes, a moment. What sort of gun?''

"Probably a MAC-10. And since George didn't hear anything, probably with a silencer. We found hoofprints—whoever used the submachine gun was riding a horse.''

"Lovely," Chesterton said, then turned back to the telephone. Desiree moved beside Track, and he held her hand. "Right, Charles, about that matter I'm interested in. Could you trouble your Company friend for a bit of casual information?" Chesterton cleared his throat. "Yes, a contract agent I should think. He used a particularly curious firearm, a MAC-10 submachine gun likely fitted with a suppressor of some sort. And the chap rode horseback. Yes, it is important. Do what you can. It's rather hard to reach me, I'm afraid, so I'll call you in an hour." Chesterton hung up. "Now wait and see," he said as he turned to the group around him.

19

"Hey, Colonel, looks like you had a rough telephone call."

Beal kept walking toward the aircraft, not looking at Tom Larrimer or even contemplating answering him. He had caught the Master just before the Master had left for the airport, where his private jet awaited him. The Master had sounded amused that someone else was trying to kill Track and the others. But he had not sounded amused that the attempt had evidently been unsuccessful. He had pointed out that if it was the Communists and Beal did the job, the Communists would be blamed. The Master had hung up.

No phrase like, "Good luck tomorrow," or, "Don't get too close to that explosion." Nothing like that.

Beal sat on the corner of the wooden table at the far end of the hangar, staring now toward Tom Larrimer and the stretched-out Huey UH-1D that Larrimer worked on. "That thing gonna be ready tomorrow?"

Larrimer didn't look up as he called back. "Should be. Why? You need it?"

"Don't be a smartass," Beal snapped, drawing the MAC-10 from the shoulder rig beneath his coat. It wasn't that terribly concealable, but it spoke with authority and had saved his life more than once. Mechanically he looked the gun over, saying to Larrimer, "What do you think about this, Tom?"

"What? The hangar? The aircraft? Or the job?"

"The job." He had worked with Larrimer in South Africa, fought beside him in Central America, served with him in Vietnam. Beal wondered if they were friends.

"I think it sucks, and I wouldn't be doin' it except you asked me. I don't see where blowin' up some damn fuel tanker off the coast of Mexico is helping out the CIA."

He had lied to Larrimer. "Well, I guess it's all part of some master plan. You're Catholic, you should know that the finite mind cannot comprehend the infinite."

"For birth control maybe I'll buy that—for blowin' up an oil tanker, I dunno, Beal. You sure that thing's carryin' water?"

"It's some kind of insurance scam that ties in with discrediting the U.S. Don't ask me why, I'm just a contract man, remember?"

"And wastin' these other guys is all of a sudden part of it?"

"They're the ones pullin' the scam, least that's what Uncle Sam tells me."

"Well, whatever one of Uncle Sam's nephews was on that telephone call with you—hell, I never saw you look so damned pissed off in my life."

"He's a hard guy to talk to," Beal said honestly.

"Yeah, well, like I said—"

But a voice from the far end of the hangar cut him off. "Hey, Colonel!"

Beal wanted the conversation with Tom Larrimer to end and so he called back to Forbes and the seven men with him coming through the side door of the hangar. "Johnny, we're over here!"

Beal looked up at the hangar's vaulted, skeletal ceiling. He wanted this operation to be over, then maybe he could figure a way out of the Directorate's control. But he knew there was no way. But he could be out of it mentally—a couple of bottles of whiskey, a couple of women. The women at least were cheap enough in Mexico if you knew where to look. Some other part of Mexico on the east coast. Maybe Tampico—the name had always fascinated him. There would be no Acapulco really if he understood it, if the Master had told him the truth about what would happen. A column of poisonous radioactive gas a mile high would erupt from the tanker, so heavily vapor laden it would drop within five hundred miles and clean itself from the air. The entire ocean in a radius of a hundred miles on each side of the supertanker would be poisoned. The beach would be irradiated for perhaps as long as thirty years. Acapulco would be a city of the dying.

It made his stomach churn.

And the only way to get away with it was the way he had decided on—to kill his friends before they realized what it was he had really had them do, before realizing it and surviving, before hunting him down and killing him.

In a way, it was preemptive self-defense.

Johnny Forbes and the others were nearly across the hangar floor and Beal reholstered the MAC-10, giving Forbes and the others a big grin. "You guys all set for tonight?"

"You bet, Colonel," Forbes answered, lighting a cigar as he strolled up.

Beal nodded. "We gotta have this deal tomorrow night so perfect that not even Superman could stop us." Forbes and the others laughed.

"Just like the old days," Forbes said with a smile.

Beal nodded, but it wasn't like the old days, not quite.

20

Desiree had volunteered to cook, and Track sat in the kitchen, watching her as she prepared the spaghetti sauce. Rudy, Carlo Capezzi's man had suggested spaghetti. "We went to the mattresses once, you know, Miss Desiree? Anyway, this guy Luigi made the damn best spaghetti I ever ate." He had proceeded to write down the recipe for her.

Track lit a cigarette he had mooched from George. "You sure you don't need any help?" he asked.

"I'm sure I don't need any help."

"I can make Kraft macaroni and cheese real great," Track volunteered.

"It isn't the same thing as making spaghetti and a sauce from scratch. Just relax and enjoy your drink."

Track nodded, watching her still. Rudy and Bob were on guard; Sir Abner Chesterton was on the roof with night glasses.

The door into the large, tiled kitchen swung open, and the man coming through was instantly recognizable, right down to his irritated expression. The dark chocolate-colored skin, the short, kinky black hair with a touch of gray flecked in it was unchanged from the last time he had seen it. The only change was the mustache—Miles Jefferson had never worn one when he had been in the FBI. But now he was a member of Congress...Track thought. Jefferson's leg moved stiffly as he entered the room, and he used a cane to walk. But he was no less erect. And knowing Jefferson, at least when the ex-FBI man was stateside, Track judged that the cane probably had a sword in it. Track had never known the man to travel unarmed.

Following Jefferson through the door was Zulu, towering over Jefferson as Zulu towered over most men. Zulu's face was calm, almost beaming as he leaned back against the door frame and folded his arms across his broad chest, watching the black American with apparent interest.

Track aimed his remark at Jefferson, but spoke as though he was talking to Desiree, "Hey, sweetheart—the neighborhood's changing."

"Bite my ass," Jefferson rasped.

Track stood up. "The Honorable Miles Jefferson—can I still call you Miles or do I start calling you Honorable?"

"Shut the hell up. You ever try flying on a goddamn airplane when you can't bend your left leg, and when you stretch it out into the aisle the stewardess keeps tripping over it? Of course you haven't—"

Zulu interrupted. "The two other gentlemen from Mr. Capezzi's organization are refreshing themselves and will take over for Rudy and Bob on guard duty shortly. I volunteered to spell Sir Abner, but George insisted that if someone helped him up onto the roof he could do it."

"Aww, shit," Jefferson snarled, looking at Zulu, then sitting down in one of the kitchen chairs and stretching his left leg out. Track walked past Jefferson and intentionally faked tripping over the leg. "Dammit, Track!"

Track burst out laughing and leaned against the counter top close to Desiree. "Hey, thanks for coming, Miles. You're just in time for Desiree's spaghetti alla mafiosa—"

"You realize if anybody'd made those two punks who picked me up at the airport—two of Crazy Carlo Capezzi's soldiers, come on, Track!"

"Don't forget, they vote, too—most of them, anyway. Don't pass them up. Someday you might be running for President and the Mafia vote might be critical—just another politically ignored minority, Miles. What can I tell you?"

"I know what I could tell you if she weren't here," Jefferson said as he motioned to Desiree.

Desiree laughed, saying, "I can always have Dan stick his fingers in my ears."

"You know that kinky stuff turns me on," Track told her, giving her a good-natured whack on the rear end.

She swatted back at him and missed his nose with the wooden spoon she had been stirring the spaghetti sauce with. The sauce smelled good.

Track flicked ashes from his cigarette into the sink.

"Somebody give me a drink," Jefferson said.

Track reached into the cabinet and pulled down the bottle of Scotch. "You still drink this junk?"

"Yeah, that's even my brand."

"You think this is your brand." Track grinned and reached into his hip pocket to draw out the stainless Smith Model 65 three-incher. "Now this is really your brand," he said as he set the gun on the table and shoved it across to Jefferson. "Careful, hotshot—it's loaded."

Jefferson caught the revolver before it skidded off the table and opened the cylinder, extracting one of the rounds with his fingernails. "Loaded with 158-grain lead hollowpoint .38s."

"I even got you the same sissy load the FBI uses in their .357s. See how thoughtful I am." Track grinned again.

"Why did you move from the other house?" Jefferson asked.

"Well, the neighbors were real noisy—had a barking dog, you know, and—"

"What'd you get me into besides a fake CIA operation to flush out a Commie?"

"What do you think I gave you the gun for—looks?" Track stubbed out the cigarette and lit another. That was why he would never go back to them instead of his cigars. When he had smoked cigarettes he had smoked at least two packs a day, sometimes almost twice that much.

As if she read his mind, and maybe she did, he thought, Desiree looked into his eyes, then at the cigarette. He nodded, murmuring, "Yeah, I know."

Jefferson snapped, "You gonna give me a glass, Track, or is the Scotch just for looks, too?"

"I'm sorry, Miles. I thought everybody in Congress drank straight out of the bottle." But Track reached into the cabinet and got out a tumbler, skidding it across the table toward Jefferson who was reaching for the bottle.

Zulu walked past Track and took a glass from the cupboard and then went to the refrigerator, taking a bottle of Schweppes from it.

"So what's going on? Your gunrunner lady friend, the black version of the Incredible Hulk here, that goddamned Brit Chesterton and a bunch of Mafia soldiers and that guy I met out front, Rafe something—"

"Rafe Minor. He's the head of a street gang from Chicago."

"Wonderful. Who else you got here? Genghis Khan and Adolph Hitler?"

"All we can offer you is a female Soviet scientist and an ex-KGB major—but Sergei is a hell of a nice guy and Tatiana's okay even if she is a scientist. Pretty girl, too."

"And just what are you doing down here?"

"Like I told you, or Desiree told you, really, it's a scam to flush out Hummingbird."

"The KGB number two in North America."

"Right, and through her, get to Potempkin."

"You know, there are a lot of people in the United States that aren't exactly fond of you after that business in Russia."

"Yeah, the American Communist Party and who else?"

"You're walking on thin ice, man."

"Desiree's alibiing me for all the time I was away."

"Some alibi—a gunrunner and a smuggler."

Track grinned. "Who helped save the life of the President—don't forget that part," he said.

"That's the only reason I took her phone call. I could get in hot water over this."

Track nodded. "Well, I wasn't going to mention it, but a bath might do some good, Miles. Anyway, nobody'll ever know you were down here doing your patriotic duty. They'll think you were on a congressional junket and wasting taxpayers' money. We'll cover for you." Track dropped his voice. "Yes, I saw Miles Jefferson with all those big spenders at the gambling casino. Yes, they were discussing the budget deficit. Yes, that woman in the red dress *was* an expert on the world money market." Track smiled. "We've got you covered, Miles—no sweat."

Zulu spoke. "I cannot take Major Track's pathetic humor any longer. Excuse me." He walked from the room with his glass and his bottle of Schweppes. As the door into the kitchen swung closed behind him, Desiree Goth began to laugh.

21

The phone calls from Carlo Capezzi and Chesterton's friend had come in almost back to back, Chesterton's man first. According to the CIA contact the SIS resident agent had, there was no CIA operative working in Mexico. Accepting that as a lie, he had inquired about the gun and gotten a big laugh. The CIA man had said that a mercenary colonel named Thomas Beal was in Mexico and that Beal, who had from time to time assisted the United States government, always carried a MAC-10 .45 ACP submachine gun. But if Beal had a gun down here, he was violating more laws than a stick could be shaken at. Track could sympathize with that—all the weapons Desiree had smuggled in for them were completely illegal, especially the ones in .45 caliber, since the Mexican government prohibited the caliber to all but their army.

Don Carlo Capezzi's call to Dan Track had been illuminating. Indeed, the guns had been stolen from a northern California armory some time ago. And indeed some unscrupulous persons had traded them across the border for drugs, as Capezzi had been able to discover.

The identity of the end user was known—Angelito

Garcia. The don had graciously provided Garcia's address. And Garcia was perhaps a Communist.

As to the mysterious .45 subgun, Capezzi had been even more specific. A well-known American mercenary with the last name of Beal was known to have used such a weapon on two assassinations in Central America. It was rumored that Beal had some new employer and because Capezzi's contacts had been unable to discover the name of the employer, it was assumed not to be the CIA or some syndicate faction.

As the don had been about to hang up, he had told Track, "A word of advice, my friend. This Beal person may be very dangerous because he thinks he is in the right. He has never worked for anyone unless it seemed that he served some just cause. From what I have been able to discover, he seems as skillful as you, yourself. You must be careful. I have alerted my business associates in Mexico." He had given Track a telephone number to commit to memory. The number would get him whatever equipment or personnel he needed, short of jet fighters or nuclear weapons, the don had added with a laugh.

Track hadn't laughed.

They sat around the table in the kitchen. George had remained on the roof, and Rudy and Bob's compatriots remained by the doors.

Track, Zulu, Baslovitch, Tatiana, Miles Jefferson, Rudy, Bob, Rafe Minor and Sir Abner Chesterton sat as Desiree brought the mounds of steaming spaghetti to the table and set the platter at its center.

"You're gonna love it—I lived off this shit," Rudy enthused.

Track gave him a grin.

As the spaghetti, the sauce, the garlic bread, the Parmesan cheese, the melon balls and the red wine were passed around, Zulu asked almost casually, "What is the new plan, Major?"

Baslovitch, Track realized, had learned that when Zulu used the title "Major" it was not in reference to the Russian. Track answered. "They'll have checked all the hotels, the private airfields, like that. And they knew Miles here wasn't in yet. So they'll have had guys follow Miles from the airport. By now they know we're here." Track sipped his wine. "As soon as we're through with dinner," he said, addressing them all, "Zulu, Sir Abner and I will follow up on the lead Don Carlo gave us regarding Angelito Garcia."

"What about the rest of us?" Desiree asked him.

"Rafe, you and Sergei take charge of security around here. Double the guard. Bob and Rudy, get yourselves up on the roof with assault rifles and keep George company. After I spoke with the don, I contacted his associates in Acapulco. By now they'll have a single sentry placed on that water tower about a quarter mile away from here. When trouble comes, one of you on the roof fire a flare from that HK flare gun, and the don's Mexican mafia friends will close in. Desiree, take a sheet and cut it up into arm bands—I told the don's men that white arm bands would indicate our people.

"Once the Mafia guys get here, you should have the KGB people in a cross fire. Take them out if you have to—see if you can get some of them alive, unless that's impossible. If Sir Abner and Zulu and I should fail in getting something solid out of this Angelito Garcia, then prisoners may be the only lead we'll have to Hummingbird.''

"What about this Beal chap, the American mercenary colonel?" Chesterton cut in.

"We're going to have to wait for him to come to us. It's conceivable he could have something to do with this supertanker thing and if we can defuse something there, wonderful—but then what's his interest in us?"

"It appears a third force is involved. I might suggest," Zulu began thoughtfully, "that perhaps this chap Beal was reconnoitering our position for some nefarious reasons of his own, then taken by surprise when the KGB attack began and he killed to enable himself to escape safely."

"I concur," Chesterton chimed in.

Miles Jefferson spoke. "You just got me down here for window dressing, didn't you?"

Track gave him a big smile and through a mouthful of spaghetti told him, "You got it, Miles. And you can handle a gun if it comes to that again. But I needed an unimpeachable—you'll pardon the expression—"

"Suck an egg."

"An unimpeachable stamp of U.S. government involvement. Just knowing you were coming helped, I'm sure. If it was important enough for you to come down to meet Baslovitch, then it wasn't some kind of a trap for Hummingbird. And I guess it worked."

"I feel like a cricket on the first day of fishing season."

Tatiana laughed. "That is a very cute remark."

"Thank you." Miles Jefferson smiled at her.

"Yeah, hey, I thought it was cute," Track told him.

"Hell, I thought it was real cute," Rafe Minor agreed.

"Very cute," Desiree laughed.

Track raised his wineglass. "Here's to cuteness!"

"Hear! Hear!" Chesterton exclaimed.

Track swallowed half the glass and set it down on the table. He looked at them all in turn. "Just remember something—until we get Hummingbird and use her to backtrack to Potempkin, the pressure isn't going to let up on us."

And that was not very cute at all, Track thought.

22

She was naked except for the towel wrapped around her as she stepped through the open bathroom door, the light from the bathroom sending a shaft of yellow along a ragged rectangle of the bedroom carpet. In the dimmer light over the bed, she could see Harlen Mills still sleeping. She had made him happy, and that made her feel pleasant inside; that would have to be enough, she supposed. Hummingbird walked across the room, flicking away the towel and throwing it toward the bathroom door.

She pulled on her terry-cloth robe and stepped into the matching pink slippers. Her hair was still wet and she shook it. She opened the bedroom door silently and stepped into the corridor, closing it, leaning against the knob.

She could hear the voices of the KGB team sent by Ghermanyevitch, hear the voice of Peter Scorese. It was his knock on the door that had awakened her. Running through the shower had been a means to take the time to think.

And she knew now what she would do. She walked down the hallway, throwing her shoulders back, pushing more of the wet strands of hair from her neck.

A KGB leader she knew by the code name of Archangel stood as she entered the living room, the three other men with him rising, as well. Only Scorese sat, his head almost down between his knees. He was out of his depth, she knew, but soon that would be rectified.

"Archangel."

"Hummingbird—it has been a long time."

She took his outstretched hand. "I am glad Ghermanyevitch sent you."

"It will be a pleasure to work with you again."

The formalities over, she nested in the center of the couch—it was still warm from someone else's body heat as she tucked her legs under her. She reached into the pocket of the robe and took out her cigarettes. Archangel had his lighter out for her and she let him light her cigarette, nodding as she exhaled a thin stream of gray smoke.

Archangel began. "Mr. Scorese tells us that congressman Jefferson was followed from the airport to a second beach house, and that two of the contract agents picked him up." Scorese had not told her—evidently telling Archangel indicated that Scorese considered Archangel her superior in KGB, which he was not, and was trying to make points with him.

"That is good news. This time, they will expect a full-scale assault. They will not get it. One of my local contacts indicates there have been certain movements within the Mexican Mafia in Acapulco. Evidently this man Track and his CIA associates have hedged their bet. I would venture to say that they assume that during a full-scale assault on the beach house, some sort of signal would be utilized and the Mafia personnel would close in and net our assault team. But they will not have that opportunity. It will be the six of us alone—''

"The six of us?" Scorese interrupted.

"Yes, you will accompany us, Peter—by way of redeeming your previous sins.''

"But, Hummingbird," Archangel began, "you cannot risk—''

She looked at him. Tall, built like a somewhat thinner Russian bear and with a brushy black mustache, he seemed a veritable tower of strength. And she knew his abilities—they were good. If the three men with him were handpicked, they would be good, as well. "I'll be in competent hands with you, Archangel. And when I spoke with Ghermanyevitch, it was agreed that I should personally ascertain that Sergei Baslovitch and the woman Tatiana are dead. There is only one way to personally ascertain this.''

She let herself smile, she was as good as any of them with a gun or with her hands. But she would never let them know that, because this way they would lay down their lives for hers and if they assumed too great a range of abilities on her part they might not. It was the best way. "I assume this is one of the beach houses for which we have plans—where they stay?''

"Yes," Scorese told her. His face looked ashen.

"I shall change, then we shall review the plans of the house and work out our tactics. I wish to strike just at dawn when there will be a momentary lull. Everyone in the house must die.''

"Not Jefferson! You can't kill a congressman—"

She looked at Peter Scorese and smiled. "Oh, yes we can. I knew that the frontal assault would fail, Peter. That is why I never mentioned this before. But I have arranged for the preparation of certain documents. They shall incriminate congressman Jefferson, make it appear as though he was in our employ. The documents are very good."

"Nobody'll believe that of Miles Jefferson. God, he was in the FBI for—"

She gave Peter Scorese her best smile. "You, my dear Peter, were in the CIA. I rest my case."

She stood up, bending over to stub out her cigarette. Without another word she started back toward the room she shared with Harlen Mills. If she was quiet she would not wake him while she changed, and he would sleep through the night and awaken only after her return from the beach house and the work she had to do there.

"Potempkin won't like it," Scorese called after her.

Hummingbird ignored the threat. Potempkin always liked what she liked.

23

Dan Track stood in front of the bedroom mirror, knotting the black silk tie, then pulling it up from half-mast. He had showered and changed—it would be a long night, and the shower had helped negate the effects of the red wine. He slipped the Bianchi X-15 rig onto his shoulders; the Metalife Custom L-frame was already rolled in the holster. He settled the holster comfortably and snapped it securely to his belt. The Trapper Scorpion .45 was already in the Alessi inside-the-pants holster, and he took this from the dresser top and positioned it beside his right kidney and secured the belt flap that would hold it.

He picked up the Puma lockblade folder and set it down beside the double-magazine pouch for the 8-round Detonics magazines he used as spares for the Scorpion. He took up the pouch and secured it to his belt at the small of his back.

He walked over to the bed where the jacket for his gray suit lay and picked it up. Slipping it on, he walked back to the dresser, taking the Puma knife, three speedloaders for the L-frame Smith, his wallet, his money clip and his keys and distributing the objects among his pockets.

Track gave himself one more look in the mirror. With the coat open, nothing really showed.

Satisfied, Track walked to the door, opened it and turned toward the mezzanine overlooking the main floor of the house. He stood there a moment. Zulu and Chesterton, Zulu in expensive sport clothes, Chesterton in a khaki suit and wearing a matching straw fedora, stood in the sunken living room.

Beside them on the floor were three G.I. mechanics' tool bags. Track knew the contents of each—one Uzi, three spare 32-round magazines for the subgun, a Walther P-5 with silencer and one spare magazine, and a box of fifty rounds of ammunition for each man's personal weapons.

Chesterton looked up, taking off his fedora and wiping his brow with the back of his hand. "Ready, Dan?"

Track nodded. He was never really ready for something like this, but it went with the territory. He started down the stairs, Desiree coming from the kitchen, the dish towel apron gone, the sleeves of her gray blouse rolled down, her high heels back on, her hair looking freshly brushed. What worried him was that over her arm she carried a maroon jacket that matched her skirt.

Track took the steps more quickly. "What the hell are you doing?"

"I'm going with you, and don't argue. It makes sense. A woman can get away with a lot of things a man can't. I won't be in the way, and with you and Zulu and Sir Abner along, I'm sure I won't be in any danger."

Track exhaled long and hard. It was useless to argue. And she was right anyway.

SIR ABNER DROVE the midnight-blue Mercedes sedan. Zulu sat beside him, and Track and Desiree sat in the back seat with tool bags on the floor between them. In the reflected moonlight, Track watched as Desiree checked her little stainless .38 special snubby, then returned it to her purse. She wasn't very talkative, and finally, after they reached the beach road and started toward town he asked her, "What's wrong? I give in too easily and you don't respect me anymore?"

She laughed, then leaned against him, putting her head on his shoulder. "I'm worried about George. I went up on the roof—"

"What did George do or say that worried you?"

"He seems despondent."

"He is, I think."

"What can we do about it?"

"How about I solve the national debt while we're at it, hmm?"

"I'm serious, be serious." He felt her hands squeeze his arm. "I want to help him," she almost whispered.

"So do I. But I don't think I can. I think he needs out. The famous team of Beegh and Track may not be a team much longer. I think he's going to take a vacation from it for a while. Give him some time to sort things out."

"He's so young."

"He's not that young. He's got to decide what he's

doing with his life and then do it. And I don't blame him. This is a damn stupid occupation.''

"After you get Potempkin, what then?''

"Want a partner in the illegal-arms trade?" he said with a laugh.

"If that's what you want,'' she answered, her tone serious. "I can quit. You've told me before and you were right—I have enough money to live very comfortably for several lifetimes. For both of us.''

Track let out a long breath. "You know I can't live off your money.'' And then he brightened, "But, on the other hand, I have most of the money the Consortium ever paid me. If you want to be a full partner, I can open up the best VIP protection outfit the world has ever seen.''

"If that's what you want, all right. I just want us to live in peace.''

"Instead of pieces,'' Track said. "I don't know if I've ever lived in peace. Peace doesn't seem to follow me. The other thing does, though.'' He laughed, squeezing her hands harder against him under his hand.

"I want to marry you,'' Desiree whispered.

"Funny, I was going to say the same thing.'' In the few shafts of moonlight that filtered now into the back seat of the Mercedes, Dan Track took Desiree Goth's face in his hands and he kissed her mouth very hard.

THOMAS BEAL put down the night glasses. "Shit! Let's go.'' Beside him, Tom Larrimer took off in a run for the 1978 Ford LTD with the interceptor engine in it, and Beal followed him. The car was parked along the beach road about five hundred yards from the house. The Mercedes wouldn't be that hard to catch—it was heading into the city. And Track was the one the Master had given specific orders to kill.

He beat Larrimer to the LTD and jumped in through the open front passenger door. Larrimer half dived into the back seat. Beal told Forbes to get the car moving as he picked up the microphone for the CB radio to contact the car a quarter of a mile down the beach road where the other six men were. "This is Stalker One, repeat, Stalker One. Subject proceeding toward city. Catch up to us. Prepare to intercept late-model midnight-blue Mercedes Benz sedan. Stalker Two—you copy?"

"Copy, Stalker One. A big ten four, good buddy."

"Cut out the crap," Beal said, and he put down the microphone.

"Blue Mercedes, right?"

"Right, Forbes."

"How many?"

Larrimer answered from the back seat. "Three men and a woman. The big black guy called Zulu, the Englishman Chesterton, this Major Track and the gunrunner dame, Desiree Goth."

"I don't like the idea of shootin' a dame," Forbes volunteered.

"I don't like the idea of these people being out to fuck the United States, Forbes—what's it gonna be?"

Beal waited.

"All right, we kill the dame, too," Forbes said nodding his head. The roar of the interceptor engine increased.

24

To the east of the city lay the wall of mountains that all but separated Acapulco from the coast, from the seaside that had made the city a rival to the Riviera. And it was in the mountains that Angelito Garcia, gunrunner, smuggler and entrepreneur, had his home.

With Desiree accompanying them, the plan Track had originally had for bulling his way into Garcia's compound had slightly changed—but he kept it on the back burner. Desiree had dealt with Garcia in a manner of speaking once, as a competitor.

She felt certain he would allow her through the gates, and once past the gates, Track had every intention of firing up the plan on the back burner.

The Mercedes slowed, Zulu intoning in a low whisper, "Four men with no visible weapons—which likely means MAC-11s or mini-Uzis under those Windbreakers they're wearing."

"Agreed." Track nodded into the mirror, watching the set of Zulu's face.

The Mercedes stopped, and Zulu got out. Iron gates set in stone pillars blocked the road to the paved driveway beyond. Bright lights were visible in the house at the top of a low hill at the end of the drive. A man stood on the opposite side of the gate. Zulu called out, *"¡Este camino esta cerrado! Soy Señor Zulu. Señorita Desiree Goth quiere hablar con el Señor Garcia, por favor. Mira—el Señor Garcia esta dormiendo. Llame Señor Garcia mañana."*

Desiree stepped out of the car. Track's reaching across to stop her was too late to do any good. He stepped out as well now. Desiree started forward, saying, *"Soy la Señorita Goth. ¿Diga me, esta Garcia en la casa?"*

"Si, señorita, pero—" the guard began.

"Nada mas—no tenga miedo, hombre. Garcia es mi amigo. Estos hombres estan conmigo. ¡Llama a Garcia—ahora!" Desiree said firmly.

The man behind the grillwork nodded slowly, then pointed toward the Mercedes. *"Apaga su motor."* Desiree turned to Chesterton, nodding. The motor cut off.

"Saca las llaves del carro," the gateman called out. Track guessed the man felt he was on a roll.

"Leave the keys right where they are, Sir Abner," Track snapped. Then he looked at the man behind the grillwork. Track started walking toward him. *"Escucha, hijo de puta. ¿Ayudeme, huh? Nosotros queremos hablar con Angelito Garcia ¿Entiende? Vete a buscarlo—toma el teléfono y llama a Garcia—pronto."*

The guard started reaching under his coat. Dan Track reached faster, the Metalife Custom L-frame springing into his right hand. He aimed between the verticals of the gate right at the man's head. *"Pon las manos donde las puedo ver, amigo—ustedes, tam-*

bién.'' Track nodded toward the other three men—none of them had his gun out yet. *"Dámela despacio."* Then Track nodded toward the left side of the man's Windbreaker. He couldn't remember how to say "submachine gun" in Spanish, so he made it up. *"La pistola machina—vamonos."*

Beside him now, Zulu had a Browning High-Power trained through the gate. Desiree was starting forward, laughing as she said, "So much for diplomacy, hmm?"

The man nearest the gates opened them, and Track stepped through, telling him, *"Sus manos detrás de su cabeza—"* It was nice to know at least a little of the language of a neighboring nation, Track mused. It was so much easier to make friends. . . .

SIR ABNER DROVE THE MERCEDES slowly along the driveway, Desiree walking beside him, a .380-calibre MAC-11 in each hand, the bolts open. Track held one of the MACs and his revolver, Zulu the fourth MAC-11 and his Hi-Power. The four guards, hands on their heads, walked in front of them. There might be more guards at the house—certainly one or two, Track had decided, possibly another four.

They kept walking. The doors leading into the house opened just beyond the veranda flooding the brick porch in yellow light. Four men rushed out, submachine guns at the ready in hard assault positions.

"No se mueva," Track commanded.

But then Desiree's voice. *"¿Habla inglés?"*

The man nearest the door called back, *"¡Sí!"*

"Then tell Angelito Garcia that Desiree Goth is waiting and she doesn't like to wait—and be quick about it."

The man hesitated, then turned toward the doorway, bumping into the enormous stomach of a man wearing walking shorts and an Hawaiian shirt who now stood blocking the light. "Señorita Desiree! Had I known you were coming—"

"You would have baked a cake?" Track asked.

It was obviously Angelito Garcia and the fat man ignored the remark. "What can I do for you at such a late hour, Señorita Desiree?"

"My associates and I are thirsty and weary of the late-night Acapulco traffic."

"Then, please, *mi casa es su casa.*"

"A penny saved is a penny earned," Track interjected.

Garcia fired a string of commands in Spanish too rapid for Track to catch, but the four men with their hands behind their heads lowered their hands slowly and walked to the side of the driveway. The four men at the doorway lowered their weapons and fanned out along the porch.

Track asked, "Do you speak English fluently, Señor Garcia?"

"Of course, gringo."

"I like you, too. But remember something—any activity from *Los Retardos*—" he gestured to the four subgun armed men "—and you get it first—right?"

Again Garcia fired a string of commands and the MAC-11s disappeared under Windbreakers and the men moved farther out along the porch.

Track smiled as he said, "Thank you very much." Desiree, Zulu beside and slightly behind her, was already moving up the front steps. Track waited as Chesterton got out of the Mercedes, then started up the steps. After taking the guards at the gate, Track and Zulu had shifted the bags with the extra weapons into the trunk of the car.

As Track moved through the doorway, he handed the MAC-11 he held to Garcia. "Here—it's very nice but I already have a submachine gun." He went inside. The lights were bright enough to perform brain surgery, Track thought.

"Please—to the end of the hall. We can all make ourselves comfortable," Garcia intoned.

When Chesterton was through the doorway, Garcia closed the door and waddled after them, a pleasant smile creasing his face.

Track reached the end of the hallway and froze. "Desiree!" he yelled.

A burst of subgun fire ripped across the floor near his feet, and as Track reached for one of his guns a voice rang out. "This is Thomas Beal, Major Track. Aside from the fact that I outrank you, I also outgun you and outman you—freeze!"

Track ignored the advice and looked behind him. One of the closet doors had opened and two men had stepped out, submachine guns in their hands.

Zulu held his pistol and his borrowed subgun—unmoving. Desiree stood close beside him. Chesterton smiled, saying, "I suppose you're the kind fellow who killed those KGB chaps at the beach house—I mean, that is a MAC-10 with a silencer you're holding, isn't it?"

"Drop your weapons," Beal shouted.

Track eyed the man. Beyond the MAC-10 held almost subconsciously in the man's hands was the face— cold, set like rock, the eyes gray under dark brows. Beal had "professional" written all over him in bold capital letters and embossed. "You're going to kill us, anyway. May as well make it more sporting when you do."

"Suit yourself, Major."

"Tell me, Colonel," Track said, starting forward slowly, noticing the other four men at the far end of the living room. A fifth man stood at the top of the stairs, an M-16 in his hands. Counting Beal himself and the two men who'd come out of the hall closet made eight men. Garcia had the MAC-11 Track had given him. And there were eight men outside. That made seventeen.

Track called out to Beal, "Let's get a few answers first, okay, Colonel? One vet to another—what do you say?"

"I don't have all night," Beal said as he walked across the living room and sat on the couch, crossing his legs, the MAC-10 going across his lap, a smile on his face.

"Fine," Track replied as he turned, very slowly, and faced Garcia. Garcia held his MAC-11 like an overweight child would hold a dripping ice-cream cone on a hot day—as if he didn't know what to do with it. "Okay, Angelito. Who did you steal or loan the M-16s and the Uzis to, the one from the northern California arsenal robbery?"

"Tell him," Beal called from behind Track.

Garcia shrugged, walking past Chesterton and then Desiree and Zulu and walking slowly toward Track. "I sell to whoever has the money. But in this case, the KGB, I think—an auburn-haired woman who looked North Americana, pretty. I saw her when we delivered and I went along for my money. I was curious about it."

Track nodded. "Ever see her before?"

"The curious thing, I did and I didn't, you know. The body looked *magnifico*, but her hair color was wrong."

"Hummingbird ring a bell?"

"Ha—maybe," Garcia said with another belly laugh.

Track nodded again. "Where did you drop the guns?"

"A house in the city. I don't remember." Garcia smiled, dragging out the last word.

"Well, I can understand that—you must be busy," Track said.

Then Track turned to Beal. "How did you find us?"

"We saw you leaving the beach house." Beal snorted. "My orders said to get you was most important, so we gave up on hitting the house and followed you. After a while, I figured the only place you could be heading, so we cut ahead of you. Forbes here," Beal said, gesturing to the man on the staircase with the M-16, "used to live in Acapulco for a while. Executive-protection job—got to know the city like a taxi driver, you know."

"And who are you working for?"

The one Beal had called Forbes called from the staircase, "The Company, mother."

"I say," Chesterton began. Track didn't look away from Beal. "I shouldn't think that's entirely accurate. Any of you know Charles Tarleton-Jones?"

"British SIS," Forbes snapped back.

"You are well informed. Well, according to Charles, who's never wrong, as you probably know, Colonel Beal isn't working for the CIA."

"It's a top-secret operation," Beal snapped rather too quickly. Track had an idea.

"I don't think so—but I bet it's got something to do with that supertanker, huh?"

Beal's face was like a rock, but Forbes dropped his jaw.

Beal was good, Track decided. "So you're admitting it—want a clean conscience before you go, huh?" Beal was smiling now. "Yeah, it has to do with the supertanker—your plans to pull some goddamn scam and screw Uncle Sam. But we're taking you out. And that tanker's never making it to California."

Desiree spoke. "How do you plan to stop a supertanker?"

Forbes spoke up. "It won't hurt tellin' you, lady, the big sucker's goin' sky high—and that cargo of water is goin' right to the bottom."

"Scam, you say," Chesterton started. "A supertanker full of water. An insurance swindle? How would that work? You'll forgive my fascination, but the insurance business is sort of a hobby of mine."

Track looked at Beal. "Yeah, how would that work, Colonel?"

Nothing in Beal's face betrayed him. "You tell us, Track—it was your idea."

Track smiled. "Sure, but just now I can't seem to remember." And Track turned to Chesterton, "Sir Abner, do you remember the horrible details of my nefarious master plan?"

"When one gets to be my age, Dan, one's memory isn't what it used to be." Chesterton's face creased with a smile.

"Say, Zulu, do you remember why I'd fill a supertanker with water instead of, ohh—say an experimental rocket fuel?"

"I remember, Dan," Desiree volunteered, stepping forward, her hands folded in front of her, a smile printed on her face. "That is why the rocket fuel is experimental—it's made from ordinary tap water."

"Right," Track said, nodding his head. "Talk about memory fading. There's such a shortage of water on the west coast they're shipping the water from the east coast. And if it doesn't work as water fuel, all the kind folks in Los Angeles can water their lawns with it. What a humanitarian I am."

"Why the hell is there water in that supertanker?" Forbes demanded.

"Remember my mentioning Charles Tarleton-Jones?" Chesterton asked. "Well," he went on, not waiting for an answer, "Charles's CIA chap confirms there's a rather volatile experimental rocket fuel in that supertanker, on its way to California. That's why it's passing eighty miles out. Now if you people were to blow up that—"

"Shut up," Beal snapped.

"Yeah, tell me some more about the water," Track insisted.

"Shut up!"

"When they open up," Track began, very slowly, his voice almost a monotone, "don't bother with any of the others. They'll get us, but we'll get Beal. Desiree. Zulu. Sir Abner—everything you've got right in Beal's good old center of mass."

"You're a dead man, Track."

"I'll wave down to you from heaven, Beal—or you wave up to me from hell—whichever."

Beal recovered quickly, Track gave him that. And that he wasn't ordering his men to open fire showed something, too. "You're slick, Track, but I expected that. You talk all you want. My men and I have a job to do—there're still *some* guys left who love America."

Zulu at last spoke. "Have any of you gentlemen heard of a group the British press rather affectionately dubbed the Vindicators?"

A new voice, from behind Track, said quickly. "I heard of 'em."

"Would you like our autographs," Track put in, turning to face the men. "He's the tall black man, in case you didn't guess. Chesterton, there, is one of us. The other two men are back at the house. So's the woman. And Desiree Goth supplied us with weapons, Jewish resistance contacts—the whole nine yards."

The man near the open closet door spoke again. "Colonel, it's a pack a lies, right?"

"Hell, yes!" Beal said firmly.

"Hell, no," Track shot back. "The other two men are my nephew, George, and a Soviet KGB major named Sergei Baslovitch—he saw the light. Our last job was in Leningrad, Beria prison. You know anybody in British SIS who trusts you, check it out. The Brits took the Soviet scientist and the poet. The third guy we sprung from Beria was an American, a contract man for the Company from twenty-five years ago and more. He's my brother-in-law."

Desiree spoke. "Do any of you know Hideo Otashi?"

"She's bullshitting," Beal shouted, on his feet now, the MAC in a hard assault position aimed at Track's chest.

"Do any of you know Hideo Otashi?" Desiree repeated. "Any of you? Who do you think flew us out under the Russian radar, who do you think fired the missiles that knocked out some of their helicopters? This man—" she pointed to Zulu "—was the machine gunner. And this man—" she pointed to Track "—was in the fuselage door with a machine gun. Check with the SIS."

"I know Hideo Otashi," Forbes called out.

"Yeah, so do I," another man added. "Otashi flew me out of an ambush in Rhodesia. Best fuckin' pilot I ever saw."

Desiree very slowly and calmly opened her handbag; Track thought she was going for her gun. But she extracted a notebook and said, "Call the number—my headquarters in Geneva. Tell them you spoke with me and I asked you to get Hideo's number. He's relaxing, on my money. And he's going to work for me again.''

She threw the address book onto the hassock near her, then sat down on the hassock's edge beside it. ''Any of you,'' Desiree said.

''How's he talk?'' It was Forbes.

''Like some kind of crazy American,'' Desiree replied with a laugh.

Track grinned at Beal. ''Somehow, I think the troops are defecting, Colonel.''

''Kill 'em,'' Beal shouted.

''No,'' Forbes called.

The man who had been flown out of the Rhodesian ambush by Hideo Otashi just shook his head and dropped into a squat on the floor, his submachine gun across his lap.

Track started walking toward Beal. ''Colonel, who you working for?''

Beal's face registered nothing. But he swung the muzzle of the MAC-10 toward Desiree Goth. ''One move and she's dead, Major.''

Track froze. ''Touché.'' Beal was up, moving, as Zulu interposed himself between Desiree and the subgun.

''Think again, nigger. The first six rounds are armor piercing—go right through you and right through her, for a matter of fact.''

''Move aside, Zulu,'' Desiree whispered.

Track's fists were balled tight. He could move against Beal, but would the gun go off?

"Track—understand you're real good with karate, but don't try and be a hero. Move and my finger locks on the trigger and the dame is dead meat."

"Who do you work for?" Track asked him.

"You wouldn't understand, anyway, Track. I work for the Directorate. I report directly to the Master."

Track could see Desiree's face. It had remained unmoved when the subgun had been pointed at her, but now it was white, as if she was in shock.

"You'll never get out of here alive," Track said feebly.

"Think again, hotshot," Beal snapped.

"Don't do anything, Dan," Desiree cautioned.

Track's fists opened and closed. "I'm walkin' outa here," Beal said. "I'm takin' the dame as far as the Mercedes."

"You might need the keys, old boy," Chesterton volunteered.

"Gimme," Beal said, holding out his hand. "And don't be stupid about it."

Chesterton slowly handed over the keys.

"If she isn't standing in the driveway," Track said slowly, evenly, "without a hair out of place, the world isn't big enough. Understand?"

"You can keep your squeeze, Track—all I want's your wheels."

Zulu stepped back between Desiree and the subgun for an instant. "If she is harmed, pray that Major Track finds you first."

"Zulu—I'll be all right," Desiree told him.

Zulu stepped aside.

Beal reached out and roughly took hold of Desiree's forearm, moving the muzzle of the gun toward her head. "Isn't that a bit unnecessary?" Desiree said coolly.

"Shut up." Beal started with her toward the doorway.

Track very slowly drew the L-frame Smith, then shifted it to his left hand. He drew the Trapper Scorpion and thumbcocked the hammer.

He followed as Beal marched Desiree past his men and toward the doorway. "Sir Abner," Track started, and then Track moved the muzzle of the L-frame to Garcia's nose. "Take Mr. Garcia's subgun and keep him nice and safe, huh?"

Chesterton took the MAC-11 and Track walked on.

Desiree had opened the door.

Track called out, "Garcia, tell your men to play statue—real loud and real quick."

Garcia shouted in Spanish. *"¡No se mueva! ¡No se mueva!"*

Track kept walking, Zulu beside him. Desiree and Beal were moving across the porch, slowly. The muzzle of the MAC-10 was still pointed at her head.

They started down the porch steps, walked across the driveway toward the midnight-blue Mercedes. He handed her the keys.

Track called after Beal, "Remember—she stays!"

Both pistols were raised to eye level, aimed at Beal's head—but even instantaneous brain death could allow a muscle spasm that would twitch the trigger.

Desiree unlocked the Mercedes.

"Down on your knees, honey," Beal rasped.

"Really," Desiree whispered, but she dropped to her knees, Beal sliding behind the wheel, the MAC-10 in his left fist now, the door open, the window down, the muzzle inches from her head.

Track shouted, "Remember, Beal. No buying out of it."

The Mercedes's engine purred to life, then a screech of tires pierced the night and the Mercedes started into a high-speed reverse along the driveway. Desiree threw herself down flat, and Track fired the L-frame at the windshield. As the windshield spider-webbed, the Mercedes did a high-speed reverse flick turn, then rocketed down the driveway. Track's pistols went empty in his hands, while Zulu's MAC-11 spit flame into the night.

Track was beside Desiree as she jumped to her feet.

"I could have ruined my stockings," she whispered as Track folded her into his arms. And then she said something else. "The Directorate. The Master of D.E.A.T.H.—my God. They really exist."

Track just stared at her.

25

Beal slid into the front seat of the LTD with the interceptor engine. "Drive, Tom. They set a trap for us—killed all the guys, even Forbes. I was the only one that got away."

"All the guys? But—"

"Drive, dammit," Beal shouted, turning the key in the ignition switch himself, then leaning back, the MAC-10 was across his lap. Truth always helped a lie. "I stole their Mercedes and got out of the compound. That bastard Garcia was workin' with 'em—Commies all over the place. Drive, Tom!"

"I'm driving! All of—" But the Ford shot forward, Beal feeling it as he was pressed back against the seat.

"We're movin' up the assault on the supertanker," Beal said.

"But how? The team was gonna swim up on it—"

"We're bombin' it."

"But what about the crew?"

"The bomb isn't that big. I'll build it tonight out of the charges we were gonna use. It'll start a fire, punch a hole in the bulkhead; there'll be plenty of time for the crew to evacuate. We can even put in a radio message to the Mexican coasties—"

"But Jesus, Colonel—"

"Look," Beal snapped. "Are you with me, Larrimer?"

"Yeah—" the man replied, his voice uncertain.

Beal looked at Tom Larrimer's eyes. They were frightened, the way his own eyes wanted to be....

ZULU HAD GAMBLED AND WON. He'd figured that Beal had a vehicle waiting and would leave the Mercedes nearby. Taking a car from Garcia's seven-car garage, Zulu had driven toward town along the road when he found the Mercedes, the tires had been shot out, and the keys were gone.

A 6-round burst from his MAC-11 had shot away the trunk lock, and Zulu had popped the lid. The mechanics' bags were untouched.

Throwing them into the borrowed Bentley, he had started back toward the Garcia house, leaving the Mercedes abandoned. It was finders, keepers.

DAN TRACK SETTLED THE MUZZLE of the Trapper Scorpion .45 against the tip of Angelito Garcia's nose. "*Señor*, my nephew has a problem, and somehow I feel you are the only one who can help me with it. He recently killed a man, but after the combat with the man was over and he had been beaten. He feels it was cold-blooded murder. I have a hard time dealing with his problem, though. You see, I have killed in combat, but never knowingly killed a man simply because I wanted to. However, if you don't take us to the house where you delivered the guns to Hummingbird, I'll kill you. Here and now.

And then I'll be able to help my nephew by understanding his problem more clearly.''

Track cocked the hammer of the .45.

"You do the bluff," Garcia said, his face greasy with sweat and oil.

"Try me," Track whispered through his clenched teeth. A lit cigar was clamped in the left corner of his mouth, and a thin stream of cigar smoke drifted into Garcia's face.

"I—I will take you," Garcia said finally, shrugging his shoulders.

Track never moved the muzzle of the Scorpion, but he looked away from Angelito's fat sweating face and into Desiree's clear, cool blue eyes. "He's a nice man, after all, isn't he?"

"Yes, a very nice man," she said with a smile.

Track leaned across Angelito Garcia and kissed Desiree's mouth lightly but with meaning.

FORBES SAT ON THE PORCH STEPS, staring up at the moon. Sir Abner Chesterton sat beside him.

"This Track guy's shooting us the straight shit?"

Sir Abner Chesterton felt himself smile as he replied, "Yes, he is doing that, Sergeant Forbes."

"Hell. Colonel Beal—he was more than family, ya know?"

"During World War II, likely before you were born, several of us in my outfit were captured by the Gerrys. One of our chaps, Twicky Collins, went over to them. All of us were very upset and swearing vendettas against him. But Twicky had always been very hard pressed to deal with pain. Or to deal with life.

We escaped, and we took Twicky with us. But Twicky didn't have a gun. The rest of us did. Because, of course, we didn't trust Twicky. But he managed to get his hands on a Mauser pistol and shot himself through the roof of the mouth. Sometimes men do evil things and the evil betrays them. Apparently your Colonel Beal hasn't had the decency or the cowardice to put himself out of his own and other people's misery. Will you help us?''

"Yes," Forbes said. Chesterton didn't look at the man's eyes, but he thought Forbes might be crying.

SERGEI BASLOVITCH had gotten Rafe Minor to spell him at his post and had gone to look in on Tatiana. The shot of penicillin should have reduced the risk of infection, and the wound on her arm had been only a superficial one.

He reached the head of the stairs and slowed his pace so the footfall would not awaken her. Her father had been forced to denounce her as a traitor a few weeks before leaving the Soviet Union. It had been all over *Pravda* and on television, as well.

But she had said she understood. Her father was a senior noncom, a veteran of almost thirty years military service in the Russian army and a decorated hero. She had understood why he had done it; there had been no choice.

But still it had bothered her, Baslovitch thought.

Very slowly he opened the door leading into the bedroom now, allowing only a shaft of gray light through the doorway as he stepped inside, then closed the door silently behind him. Slowly his eyes became accustomed to the darkness and the form beneath the blanket began taking greater shape and definition. After they captured Hummingbird, if they could capture Hummingbird, and she led them to Potempkin, it would be finished. Over the years in the Soviet service he had stashed away in various Swiss accounts large amounts in ill-gotten gains. A hundred and twenty-five thousand dollars in gold he had "recovered" after trailing one of Hitler's lower-echelon financial ministers. He had simply neglected to return the gold to the Soviet Union. It hadn't belonged to the Soviets, anyway, but to thousands of hapless persons who had been victimized by the war. He had taken ten percent of it and anonymously donated it to one of the various children's relief funds throughout Europe and America. The rest he had banked.

There had been twenty-three thousand pounds he had stolen from a British SIS operation in West Germany. Another ten percent to salve his conscience, another series of deposits in Switzerland.

Over the years there had been various other money making opportunities and various other deposits. He had left instructions with each bank that should he not contact them for a period of five years, he would be dead and they were to donate the money to a list of charities he had provided.

But it would provide for him now, and for her he thought as he watched Tatiana sleep.

Desiree Goth had pledged to help them establish new identities. He had always fancied wearing a beard. And he supposed Tatiana might have to dye her golden hair—that would be the worst sin of all. But she would still look lovely.

He approached the bed very slowly, reaching to touch at her cheeks, then her forehead. There was no fever.

But even in the low level of light, he could tell that she had opened her eyes.

"Go back to sleep," he whispered.

"Sergei— Is everything—"

"Everything is well. Rest now."

"I love you."

He bent over the bed and kissed her cheek, whispering, "And I love you." The novelty of being totally open, totally truthful with someone would never lose its luster to him.

HUMMINGBIRD, ARCHANGEL and Peter Scorese crouched in the sand just above the beach. The house was in easy view less than a hundred yards away. The surrounding palm trees cast darker shadows against the grayness of the dawn behind them. The three KGB men Archangel had handpicked for the mission were on the far side of the house, in position.

She looked at Archangel. In his hands was the Barnett Commando Crossbow, a hunting broadhead was cocked and ready in the flyway.

She looked at Peter Scorese. He was useless—his hands visibly trembled as he clutched the Uzi submachine gun.

Hummingbird had made her decision.

"Archangel, I will meet you down in the palm trees there—" and she pointed to her right.

"Yes, Hummingbird," the voice came back, and he was up, rolling over the ridge of sand and gone into the darkness.

"Where will I be?" Scorese whispered to her.

"Right here. Forever."

She moved the switchblade forward as she pushed the button, the blade swinging out, then hammering up beneath the sternum for the heart.

"Potempkin will—" Scorese coughed the words in a low whisper.

"I am Potempkin, Peter. And I can't say that I'm at all sorry. You have always been a very vile man. A traitor to your own country, and only for money. You have outlived your usefulness to us, and you long since outlived any usefulness to yourself.

She twisted the knife, and smelled his bowels unlock.

She wrenched the knife free and stabbed it several times into the sand to clean it of blood, and then with Scorese's Uzi in her hands she followed Archangel into the night. Scorese as an ex-CIA man would be the perfect human link to the falsified documents she had. And he had been vile.

GEORGE BEEGH WATCHED the graying horizon toward Acapulco and listened to the soft lapping of the waves against the beach behind him. The rooftop had been a wise place to spend the night. A chance to think uninterruptedly.

And his thoughts were very clear; now he knew what he would do.

Above all else he needed time with his father, and

he'd use that time to sort himself out. After killing the Russian colonel, he had given the balance of the mission only halfhearted participation.

That would cease.

He had done something wrong, killed when there had been no reason to kill. But he realized his own basic goodness. And the goodness of his cause. To rid the world of an evil—at least a significant bit of that evil.

George stood up, and his face cringed with the pain in his left leg. That would heal. On the edge of the flat roof was the Bianchi Scorpio rig with the Smith 9mm minigun. He picked it up, settling the rig across his shoulders. Then he took up the belt holster with the Colt Combat Government and strapped it on. He thumbed the black Jack Daniels baseball cap back from his forehead, picked up his M-16 and started to patrol the roof. Rudy and Bob were sitting at the far end with their night glasses.

George started toward them. And he thought only about the job.

26

Chesterton drove, Zulu beside him in the front seat
of the silver-gray Bentley. Track was beside Desiree
in the back seat. The car behind them, another Bentley, was packed with Forbes and his mercenaries.

Between Zulu and Sir Abner sat Angelito Garcia.

As they drove toward the house where Garcia had
delivered the arms, Desiree spoke loudly enough that
all could hear, ignoring Garcia's presence. "Many
years ago I was involved in an arms deal in Southeast
Asia. I had a competitor—I usually did in those days.
Zulu, do you remember?"

"Maricius Savitch—yes, I remember him."

"Savitch had double-crossed the people he had
been selling to—sold them M-16s that had been salvaged off a ship that had gone down in the sea of
China. The M-16s had saltwater damage and were
hopelessly corroded. Because of Savitch, the buyer
distrusted all arms dealers. Zulu and I fled through
the jungle for our lives, and Savitch was with us. Not
by choice, but we couldn't leave him—"

"Miss Desiree couldn't leave the man," Zulu interrupted. "She has always had a warm heart."

"Savitch, Zulu and I ran into a very primitive
tribe—I don't remember the name. Savitch was shot

with a poisoned dart. There was nothing we could do—his body was gradually being seized with paralysis and he was dying from suffocation.''

"As Savitch died," Zulu continued, picking up the story, "he told Miss Desiree and myself that he wished to somehow repay her kindness. And so he would tell her the one thing of true value that he knew. Years earlier, he had been in the employ of a rather bizarre organization. It was alternately referred to as the Directorate and as—"

"As D.E.A.T.H.—some sort of acronym," Desiree put in.

"And that their leader," Zulu said slowly, "was a man of unspeakable power. He was known as the Master of D.E.A.T.H. and was the head of the Directorate. As Savitch died, he told us that D.E.A.T.H. was centuries old, had precipitated World War II by means of various manipulations, had in part been involved in beginning the war in Vietnam. Savitch had been in their employ, balked at what he had considered a suicide mission and gone underground. His wife had been killed by a rapist who had broken into her apartment. His daughter had been run over by a truck on her way home from school. His father, who had never been ill before, had a massive fatal heart attack. Savitch found himself framed for the triple murder of police officers in a suburb of Detroit, Michigan. Listed as armed and extremely dangerous, he realized that he would be shot on sight.

"Savitch dyed his hair, shaved off his mustache, taught himself how to eat like a European rather than an American, affected an accent, killed an Austrian businessman and assumed his identity and left the United States. He changed his name several times after that. But Savitch was his real name.

"Later," Zulu continued, "Miss Desiree requested that I verify the story of Maricius Savitch, which of course I did. The deaths of his family, the accusation for the triple murder, the death of the Austrian businessman who provided his first change of identity—all this was true."

Track sat very quietly. "We're going to have to stop Beal. He'll go after the supertanker himself, won't he?" he asked no one in particular.

Desiree answered. "If you go against this Master of D.E.A.T.H., Dan—"

"We know it isn't water in that supertanker's hold. We know Beal used his own people. Which means he was planning to kill them. Rocket fuel—it could be very volatile."

"There." It was the first word Angelito Garcia had said since entering the car.

"The single-story house with the high false front?" Track asked.

"Yes."

"How many of them should there be?"

"This I do not know."

Track nodded then said, "Desiree, hit the floor. Zulu, be ready with a subgun. Sir Abner, drive right through that picture window and into the living room—these old cars are built like tanks, anyway."

"Right—" And the Bentley's engine began to

growl louder as Chesterton swerved the vehicle over the curb and across the front yard.

HARLEN MILLS ROLLED OVER. Hummingbird had said she would be gone and she was. He reached out to the spot where she had been beside him.

Then he heard the loudest noise he had ever heard, as if the house was falling down around him.

He threw his feet over the side of the bed and opened the nightstand drawer beside him, reaching for the pistol Hummingbird had left for him.

He took it into his hand, pulled on his bathrobe, and ran barefoot across the room, belting the robe.

She had said all he had to do was hold the gun tightly and pull the trigger and it would shoot.

He could hear the sounds of things shattering.

The police perhaps—or American intelligence. Perhaps Hummingbird had left valuable papers or something.

He felt sick to his stomach, but he wanted her to know that he believed in her more than the party, more than anything.

He opened the door, stepped into the corridor and started to run along its length. In three strides he saw it—a huge white European car. A giant of a black man stepping from the passenger side, a mustached man with brown hair wearing a gray suit, the man tall, lean, muscular.

"Frèeze!" Harlen shouted.

The black man turned toward him, something that looked like the guns gangsters used in movies in his hands.

Harlen Mills stabbed the pistol forward to the full extension of his arm and fired, the pistol rocking painfully in his hand.

The gangster gun made a loud rattling sound and Harlen was falling, his knees buckling, his ears ringing, a coldness in the pit of his stomach and a sharp pain in his chest. He fell until something hard slammed against him. He knew it was the wall as he rolled along it. Why were these red smears along the wall? Was it blood, he wondered.

He slumped, his head sagging against his chest.

He started to cry—it wasn't the realization of death, or the realization he had failed, because he had tried. But he would miss Hummingbird.

A woman with a pretty face, dark hair and very deep blue eyes knelt beside him. The tall, muscular man with the mustache was talking. "You're the only one here. Why?"

"Gone," Mills told the man. "Tell Hummingbird that I really did love . . . love her . . . plea—"

He could feel a light-headedness. He thought he heard the man with the gray suit saying, "I promise, promise I'll tell her."

He felt strangely good inside and very warm, and he closed his eyes.

27

There had been nothing else to do. Track had sent Chesterton, packed in like a sardine, with Forbes and his mercenaries to try to intercept Beal. Police sirens were already sounding in the distance. Chesterton's contact had known what was in the fuel tanker. A special, experimental rocket fuel that was irradiated. If the fuel was being shipped it meant only one thing—that a means of slowly emitting radiation while the fuel was burned had been achieved. It would vastly increase the yield over a comparable volume of ordinary liquid rocket fuel. Under a controlled burn it would be very safe.

But traveling in the tanker it was highly volatile because the temperature could not be kept cool enough. That was the reason for the security flap, as Tarleton-Jones had put it.

When Chesterton had hung up, Chesterton had explained it all, briefly, succinctly, then added, "If Colonel Beal causes a fire or explosion aboard the supertanker, it would be the worst environmental catastrophe ever to take place. Thousands would die. This entire area, I should imagine, would be contaminated for decades."

Track drove now, Zulu on the far side of the Volvo

they had found in the garage near the partially demolished house. Desiree crowded between them on the front seat.

He had tried calling the number of the Mexican Mafia contact, but there had been an answering machine only. It meant that even the contact was watching the beach house. He had tried calling the beach house to alert Rafe Minor, Baslovitch, and the others, but the line was dead.

They had left Angelito Garcia handcuffed to the steering wheel of his Bentley in the living room of the house, left him to explain the dead man.

They drove now. It would be up to Chesterton to stop Colonel Beal—if Beal could be stopped. At least until the situation at the beach house was resolved. Track had the speedometer up to eighty as he drove the Volvo along the beach road.

In the darkness, he could hear Zulu checking the submachine guns. Chesterton had kept two of the MAC-11s for his own use, and the subguns in the mechanics' bags were now divided one apiece, including one for Desiree.

As they drove, Zulu asked, "What is your plan, Major?"

"We'll go along the road to the beach house, then cut off the road and straight up to the house across the sand. If I keep her rolling we shouldn't get stuck." It was bright at the rim of the mountains—if an attack had not yet come, it would come soon. "If I make us conspicuous enough, even if the attack has begun we should draw a lot of fire. Zulu, why don't you climb over into the back seat, then help Desiree. You guys can fire from the side windows.''

"Yes," Zulu's voice boomed. Track could feel the balance of the sedan shifting as Zulu climbed over. Then, "Miss Desiree?"

"I should know better than to wear a skirt when I'm with you, Dan—"

"Yeah, but you've got such pretty legs."

Desiree let out a little scream, then, "Dammit—"

"I don't hear anything yet—we should be pretty close," Track told them. But he realized that the reason he heard nothing could have been that it was over. . . .

THE MORE HE WALKED, the better the leg felt—at least that's what he told himself. Using the butt of the M-16 like a cane helped, too. He had passed Bob on the landward side and was approaching Rudy on the seaward side of the roof. Rudy turned around, then in a coarse whisper snapped, "Hiya, George."

"How's it goin', Rudy."

"Can't complain."

George used the M-16 like a third angle of a triangle and leaned forward against it. "I gotta ask you something. Why that pistol of yours?"

In the gray light, George could see Rudy smile. "Not as popular now as it used to be, because a lot of people these days figure they're too good for it, ya know—but it's a family thing—what I do. My old man got me into it when I was seventeen and they needed an extra guy to just stand watch around the gates of Don Carlo's house. He had this neat place in

Connecticut. But there was what you civilians'd call a gang war. So, I pilled in the car with the rest of the guys, and son of a gun if my old man doesn't realize they were short a gun. Well—I remember it always. My old man says, 'Hey, kid—you gonna stick with this work?' And I tell him 'Sure.' So he reaches under his overcoat and he pulls out this—'' Rudy drew the Bolo Mauser from his shoulder holster. "My old man tells me, 'Don't use for nothin' but stayin' alive with, kid—*capice*?' And I tell him 'Sure.'" And Rudy laughed. "Never told me the 7.63 Mauser stuff is harder to get than a free lay at a cathouse. And I took my old man's advice. Whenever the job's called for somethin' else, always got an assault rifle or a shotgun, you know. I keep this for doin' just what he said, stayin' alive. Someday—and my kid's gonna be a doctor, you know—he's gonna have this—'' he gestured with the Bolo "—and I'm gonna tell him the same thing my old man told me 'cause it was good advice."

"You're lucky. My dad was never around."

"Yeah, Dan told us. You're lucky, though, findin' your old man after all these years. Wasn't your old man's fault he was out doin' his patriotic duty for the country and he wound up rottin' in some Commie prison all these years. Be lucky you got him, George. My old man passed away, God rest his soul, a dozen years ago. And I think about him now sometimes—times like this."

George reached out his hand in the darkness and clapped Rudy on the shoulder. "Hey, George, you and your old man take every day you got, you know?''

George only nodded.

George heard a single pistol shot, and he wheeled toward the landward side of the roof, the M-16 in his hands, his leg feeling on fire as he moved. Bob was falling and something was protruding from his back, visible in the gray light.

"Crossbow, kid!" Rudy reached behind him as George looked toward him for an instant. The flare pistol. He raised it and fired, George already starting to run toward the fallen syndicate man on the far side of the roof, his leg screaming at him. He heard a whooshing sound, but it wasn't the flare, and he threw himself to the cinder surface of the roof.

George rolled, the M-16 gone, his hands over his head, the impact hammering at him like a massive fist, and he realized he was screaming against the noise.

He was up on his knees. He saw the flash now, the smoke. "Mortars!" he screamed.

As the whistling sound increased, he could hear the crack of the Bolo Mauser, and he looked back toward Rudy as he threw himself down.

The mortar hit, and George's body rocked with it. And then he felt a sick feeling inside—he was falling and he opened his eyes as he plunged downward. Smoke and dust and debris surrounded him. He shot his hands out, and his left shoulder hit something hard. He rolled with it, as things hammered at his back and his legs. Something cracked into his head, and blackness started to invade his mind. He fought it, lurching forward onto his knees, choking in the dust and smoke.

He was on the second-floor landing of the house, but barely—another foot or so and he would have fallen all the way from the roof to the first floor and broken every bone in his body. But he could still move and he slumped against the rail. He was up, the Smith minigun coming into his left hand with an awkward but positive draw from his right-handed shoulder rig. The Colt Combat Government .45 was in his right hand. He guessed Rudy had bought it on the roof.

So he owed the KGB for something else. . . .

28

Track cut the wheel hard left and took the Volvo off the road. Downshifting for traction, then accelerating. There was a mortar in operation, and the beach house seemed to be shrouded in smoke, tongues of flame leaping upward into the gray sky. He aimed the Volvo straight for the mortar, already hearing the sounds of Zulu's subgun behind him.

Track reached to the seat, picking up the third subgun, frictioning the wheel of the Volvo as he worked open the bolt, then shifting the subgun to his left hand, the wheel in his right. He frictioned the wheel again as he upshifted, then regrasped the wheel, firing the subgun toward the mortar. There were three men there, one of them firing an assault rifle. The windshield of the Volvo spiderwebbed and cracked, a chunk of it blowing in on the right-hand side.

Track hammered his right foot to the floor, and the Volvo's engine roared. The mortar team was close now, and he shouted, "I'm ramming it!"

Track let go of the wheel, both hands on the subgun now as the Volvo bounced upward, slamming into the mortar tube and plate. A body was thrown up over the hood and smashed through the windshield. The driver's door sprung open, and Track stomped on the brake, firing the subgun, the roar of the two other subguns making his ears ring, hot brass pelting at his face and neck.

The Volvo lurched, skidded and stopped, glancing into the trunk of a palm tree. Track's body shuddered.

He half rolled, half fell from the driver's seat.

Subgun fire ripped toward them from the palms. Track fired his weapon as Zulu shouted, "Major—hold fire!"

Track snapped up the subgun's muzzle and Zulu rolled from the back seat. Desiree fired over him as Zulu came up to his knees, the subgun clenched in both mighty fists, spitting flame into the knot of palm trees.

The man in the palm trees went down. Track started ramming a fresh magazine into the butt of his subgun, but the sand beside him erupted and the rear windshield of the Volvo shattered and Desiree screamed....

GEORGE WAS STARTING DOWN THE CORRIDOR. Behind him, he heard Baslovitch calling for Tatiana.

George didn't say anything, but forced himself to run. The knee wound had opened up and his left leg was drenched with blood now. As he reached Tatiana's doorway, the door opened. George drew back, both pistols ready.

Tatiana, dirty, smoke belching from her room, staggered through.

George caught her as she fell toward him, and then Baslovitch was beside him. "Here, George." The

Russian set down the SPAS and the bag of shotgun shells and caught Tatiana in his arms as easily as a child might pick up a doll. "The main floor's on fire, and we're being pinned down by sniper fire. We can't get out."

"Shit," George snarled, grabbing his uncle's shotgun and the bag of ammo. The .45 was holstered now, the SPAS slung under his right arm, the bag under his left, the minigun shifted to his right fist.

He limped after Baslovitch along the corridor and toward the stairs leading to the main floor.

"Rafe Minor caught a piece of window glass in his right arm," Baslovitch said. "He's bleeding badly but if we can get him out, he'll live. The other two Capezzi men—one of them was on fire and the other tried putting him out. That's when the sniper fire started and both of them caught it. Miles Jefferson and Rafe are returning fire. The mortars have stopped—might be Dan—but whatever crashed into the mortars is pinned down, too."

"Where the hell are these Mexican Mafia guys?"

"I don't know, but they'd better hurry. The rest of the roof's going to go. How are Bob and Rudy?"

"Bob's dead, I know. I think they got Rudy, but I couldn't see." They were navigating the stairs now, picking their way through the burning rubble. "The roof caved in and I fell through."

"You're lucky to be alive," Baslovitch called over his shoulder.

The smoke was getting heavy now, and George choked on it. As they got closer to the foot of the stairs, they began to hug the wall. Sniper fire hammered through what had been the windows, and flames licked up from the first floor along the stairwell.

Tatiana was stirring. "The bastards," Baslovitch shouted. "The mortars with these incendiary rounds were to make the place into an inferno—and then snipers to keep us inside. The bastards."

They reached the bottom of the stairs. Baslovitch was stooped now, hugging the wall, still carrying Tatiana.

George licked his lips. He'd get out of it—somehow. His uncle was right, people who did things like this had to be stopped no matter what the cost. . . .

HUMMINGBIRD HOISTED THE DRAGUNOV to her shoulder again and sighted through the sniper scope, settling on what looked like a man carrying a woman—it would be Baslovitch and the defecting female scientist who had helped him. Hummingbird fired. Smoke billowed up suddenly as more debris fell through the roof, and she couldn't see if she had scored a hit.

The machine gun beside her roared again, chunks of the stucco exterior of the beach house disintegrating as Archangel did his work.

"Keep them down by the automobile. That looks like the Volvo we had at the house. If they killed Harlen—" But she didn't finish it, could not have finished it. The machine gun opened up again. Hummingbird glanced to her left—more of the Volvo was shredding under Archangel's gunfire.

She refocused her attention on the house, firing the Dragunov again. It would only be minutes until the entire structure collapsed and all within it died. And then she would kill this man Track, because inside her she felt the hollowness that told her Harlen Mills, the only person in her adult life she had ever really cared for, had to be dead. She pulled the trigger again and again.

TRACK HANDED HIS SUBGUN to Zulu. "You can handle two of these. After the next burst from the machine gun, return fire as heavily as you can—you and Desiree."

"Be careful, Dan," Desiree called from beside Zulu.

"Look, kid, we're gonna make it out of this together, and we might even take our little boy here along," Track patted Zulu on his bald head.

"Major—just get out of here!"

Track laughed as the machine gun opened up again, what was left of the Volvo's glass shattering now, and as the machine gun died, Zulu pushed up, firing both subguns, Desiree beside him. With a pistol in each hand, Track ran for it, into the palm trees, jumping the body of the dead man, grabbing up the man's Uzi as he stashed the Scorpion into his right hip pocket.

He kept running, as sniper fire from the Dragunov came at him, taking chunks out of the palm trees.

Above him he heard helicopters crossing the darkness of the water—either police or the Mexican Mafia people.

Track threw himself down, rolling onto his back. He took the white handkerchief from his hip pocket and tied it around his left biceps, then picked up the subgun and the revolver. With any luck Desiree would do the same and so would Zulu. He kept running through the palm trees, toward the machine-gun nest and the sniper.

A helicopter skimmed the sand, and Track squinted at it as the machine hovered over him. Then a voice cracked over a PA, "Señor Track?"

Track waved his arm so they could see the handkerchief arm band, then pointed the subgun toward the machine-gun nest."

The helicopter veered off, and two more closed with it and started a low pass over the machine-gun nest.

And Track could see the machine gunner rising to his feet, his weapon held at his side, firing skyward, tongues of yellow licking into the gray light.

Track threw the subgun to the sand and steadied the L-frame in both fists. He double-actioned it once, then again and again, emptying the revolver as the machine gunner's body rocked with hits.

And then the machine gunner crumpled and fell.

Track caught sight of a running figure dressed in black, and a sniper rifle being cast into the sand.

It would have to be Hummingbird. Track broke into a dead run, holstering the empty revolver, snatching the Trapper Scorpion from his right hip pocket.

Two of the helicopters flanked her now, Track shouting, "No! No!"

Subguns at the fuselage doors opened fire, the running figure's body twisting, sprawling forward into the sand as the helicopter passed over.

Track kept running, skidding to the sand on his knees beside the figure.

He rolled the body over—his hands already sticky with blood. The watch cap fell from the head, and auburn hair cascaded down.

The eyes opened a moment. "You're Hummingbird?" Track asked.

"Harlen?" a weak voice asked.

"He said to tell you he loved you," Track said.

"Track? Congratulations."

"Who is Potempkin?" Track asked, gently but firmly.

The eyes closed and blood trickled from her mouth as her teeth gritted together.

"I am Potempkin—" and her head lolled back. The eyes stared up at him until he pressed his thumbs over them and worked down the lids.

29

Zulu, George, Miles Jefferson and Desiree were with him in the Bell Long Ranger II 206 L-1 helicopter. The Mexican Mafia pilot was saying, "It will take less than three minutes, Señor Track."

"Gracias."

"Just hope to God Sir Abner nailed that guy, Beal," George shouted.

Zulu and George were loading magazines for the Walther subguns, Desiree holding her skirt up like a basket, 9mm solids filling it. Track was checking the SPAS-12.

The other two helicopters were still visible heading out to sea to evade the police, carrying in them the survivors of the house. Bob had died, and his body had not been recovered. The bodies of two other Capezzi men—the one who had burned to death and the other who had been shot trying to save him—had not recovered, either. Rudy, still holding his Bolo Mauser clenched in his right fist had been burned and had two broken legs. But the burns were minor, and he would live. Track thought of the man—a likeable guy despite his profession. As they had picked his body out of the rubble, he had opened his eyes and said to George, "Don't let 'em throw away my sport coat—all my stripper clips—can't get 'em no more.''

George had spent another ten minutes searching the rubble. The sport coat was shredded but the loaded stripper clips for the Bolo had been salvaged.

Baslovitch and Tatiana were in another helicopter with the wounded Rafe Minor. The medic with the Mexican Mafia people had been able to stop the bleeding and Rafe would make it.

Police cars were visible everywhere, along all the arteries to the beach. Track conjectured it would be considered some terrorist action linked to the supertanker and he hoped this thought wouldn't prove prophetic.

The helicopter was already starting down, a small airfield on the far northern edge of the city visible like a large postage stamp. Track's stomach was telling him something—"Hurry it up, *compadre*."

"*Bueno.*" The pilot grinned, the helicopter starting to descend more rapidly now. In the distance he could see flames, a hangar afire, nearly gutted, and on the dirt road leading to the field, a fire engine was coming.

The helicopter began its approach, skimming over the airfield, and as it touched the ground, Track jumped from the machine, running toward the hangar. He stopped as he saw a figure slumping from the side of the partially charred Bentley.

He changed direction and ran toward it and saw Sir Abner Chesterton, his face blackened in spots, his right arm limp. The Englishman opened his eyes as Track cradled his head back. "Dan...booby trap... the entire hangar went up...Forbes and all the others. A body inside was the booby trap. Forbes called the man Larrimer. The helicopter pilot. But the helicopter was gone. I crawled to the car...try to...try to—"

"Rest easy," Track said, hugging Chesterton's head to his chest.

"Dan?"

It was Desiree.

"Sir Abner—is he—"

"Alive," Track replied. "I don't know how much longer. Zulu, you and Desiree get him away from here. Find a doctor. I'm taking George and Miles and we're going out to that supertanker to stop Beal."

Desiree knelt beside him now, and he felt her lips brush his cheek. "I love you."

Track closed his eyes a moment. "Take care of my buddy here." Track kissed her lips quickly as he shifted Chesterton's head to her arms.

And then he started to run, the SPAS slung under his right arm, the ammo bag under his left. Beal was going to die, Track decided....

GEORGE WAS BESIDE HIM in the open fuselage of the chopper, the Mexican Mafia pilot at the control. Miles Jefferson was closing the cylinder on his Smith revolver. Above the rotor noise as they skimmed mere feet over the waves, Jefferson shouted, "You realize what kinda trouble I can get in—me, a congressman?"

"Nobody said you had to come along—I just asked, Miles," Track shouted.

"Yeah, well, go to hell—after we nail this son of a bitch!"

Track clapped Jefferson on the shoulder, then began to unlimber the SPAS. His plan was the only one he could think of—overtake the chopper Beal flew and shoot him down. The helicopter was not equipped with missiles or any actual weaponry. It was the sort of thing businessmen used, but in other businesses besides killing.

Track picked up the radio headset to be in contact with the pilot. "You see anything, Emilio?"

"No, *señor*. Wait, something is coming over the radio—" And Emilio patched him in—static. Then Emilio's voice. "I hear something, *señor*, a signal—"

And now Track could hear it. The transmission was weak but getting stronger by the instant. "Track? This is Beal. Over."

Track spoke into the headset microphone. "Turn back, Colonel. Over."

"Fuck off. When I hit these explosives that ship's goin' up like a Roman candle. A cloud a mile high, loaded with radiation. Everything for at least a hundred miles in all directions is gonna be loaded with radiation. Turn back or you and your friends are dead. Over."

"What about you, Beal? You going to die for this Master of Death crudball? Over."

"This helicopter is specially fitted and I'm wearing antiradiation gear and breathing from a contained air supply. I drop my explosives and just fly away, land the chopper and walk off—simple as that. Over."

"What about your men? You couldn't have

planned that booby trap all along—or did you hire them just to get after us? Over."

"Negative on that Track. This is an alternative plan. Nobody knew about the radiation gear except me. The special fitting on the chopper was to guard against chemicals in the explosive cloud from the ship's fuel supply. My guys were gonna swim up and plant their charges—trouble for them was that the timers were all built to blow ten minutes before the time for which they set."

Track licked his lips as Beal's voice grated on. "You can't beat the Directorate. The Master controls so much that if you go against him you'll never be able to close your eyes at night, you'll never be safe, the people you love will get it, everything bad that can happen to you will happen—I know. I tried buckin' him when they first hired me. It's no good. One vet to another, like you said at Garcia's house—get outa here. Beal out."

"Beal! Beal! Do you read me? Beal!"

The radio was dead.

Track raised the Aimpoint 8x30s and stared out across the ocean. He could see the helicopter—it was distant but clear. "Emilio—you read me?" he said into his headset.

The pilot's voice came back. *"Sí, señor."*

"How much speed you got left in this thing?"

"Another fifty miles per hour, *señor*, but we will not have enough fuel to return to shore if we increase our speed."

"Did you follow the conversation, Emilio?"

"*Sí, señor*. I have a wife and two children in a suburb of Acapulco."

"We don't stop Beal, they're dead."

"*Sí, señor*. I have not gone swimming in the ocean in a long time—always too busy, ha!"

The rotor noise began to increase almost imperceptibly. Track stared down at the water, the effect of it racing away beneath him almost mesmeric. He thought of Desiree. The helicopter didn't have a life raft. If Emilio could set the chopper down right, it might float for ten minutes. And if they missed with Beal, they could not outrun the radioactive cloud that the explosion of the rocket fuel would raise.

He told himself he'd survived worse, and he tried to remember what was worse—but memory failed.

"George, if we don't make it out, well—"

"I know," George shouted back, grinning. "It's been worth it."

He looked at Miles Jefferson. "We can always try settin' her down on the supertanker. Relax, I'm feeling more optimistic by the minute."

"Don't worry—and the hell with you," Jefferson said with a laugh, clapping Track's shoulder. "But I tell you, it's been interesting. And swimming's supposed to be good for my leg. Probably help out your crazy nephew there, too."

"Beal's got a bomb and he's going to drop it, send up a radioactive cloud and release a radioactive fuel spill into the sea. He's got special gear, protective clothing—stuff like that."

"All we've got is Yankee ingenuity," Jefferson said. "Let's go for it."

"Right on!" George shouted.

Track scanned with the binoculars again. Not only could he see the chopper ahead, but he could also see the supertanker. If Beal dropped his bomb, they'd shoot him down, anyway.

"Emilio, you holding back at all?"

"It's just another five or ten miles. . ."

"Let's have everything!" Track shouted.

"Sí, señor. Suerte, huh, to all of us?"

"Suerte, amigo," Track said into the microphone.

He folded out the stock of the SPAS-12, resetting the sling. George held his Combat Government in his fist. Miles Jefferson had an M-16.

Track worked off the safeties—the big SPAS was ready. He hoped he was.

"Emilio, get us as close as possible.

Beal's chopper was starting to descend. Ahead, the supertanker was cutting through the Pacific, white froth splitting off its massive bows, the whitecaps visible beneath the chopper snapping high. The air was cool to the point of being cold. Track shouldered the SPAS. Jefferson and George lay prone on the floor of the chopper.

Track shouted, "George—aim for the fuel tanks! They're a bigger target for your pistol! Miles, go for the main rotor!"

"What the hell you doing just giving orders?"

"The bubble, Miles—I'm goin' for Beal. Get us twenty-five yards from her, Emilio!"

"But *señor*, if the helicopter should explode. . ."

"I know—do it."

"*Sí, señor*, but I will have only one chance—the machine moves very fast."

Beal's chopper was starting the pass for the super-tanker. Beneath the aircraft Track could see explosive pods, bombs of some type.

The two machines flew parallel now. As Beal's machine started to climb for the pass, Emilio was mirroring it's movement. Closing the gap. A hundred yards. Fifty yards.

The tanker was less than a quarter mile distant. "Now or never, Emilio!" Track shouted.

The chopper lurched under them, and suddenly the distance was cut to twenty yards.

"Fire—now!" Track yelled over the noise of the engine.

Track began working the trigger of the SPAS, hot brass from George's .45 pelting him, the roar of the 3-round bursts from Jefferson's M-16, the SPAS bucking at Track's shoulder.

He could see Beal turning to stare at them. Track fired again and again and again, and Beal's helicopter suddenly vanished inside a ball of flame. Emilio veered their machine away, the heat of the fireball scorching Track's hands as he drew back. The Plexiglas on the port side of the Mexican Mafia chopper was stained black. The chopper was skimming so close to the water now that spray lashed up at them. Under the force of the secondary explosion, Beal's high explosives, the chopper rocked and Track was thrown back from the fuselage door, the SPAS falling from his hands.

"Some of the debris has hit our main rotor! We are going down!" Emilio yelled.

Track held his breath as the machine trembled around them. Ahead was the supertanker. If they crashed in the path of the tanker, they would be dead.

They missed the bow of the supertanker by yards, the helicopter stuttering, waves washing up over the fuselage doorframe, the chopper rising now. "Hold on!"

Track slammed aft, then rolled forward. The chopper went down.

When he looked up, they were on the water and he smelled burning aviation fuel.

He threw away the SPAS-12—the gun would just weigh him down.

George stood unsteadily at the fuselage door. "Jump for it!" Track shouted, throwing him a life vest. Jefferson was already climbing into one.

Track grabbed a third, and then he looked forward. "Emilio!" he called.

Track shoved George into the water and then started forward. The smell of the burning fuel was chocking him, as he caught sight of Emilio. The right side of the pilot's face was smeared with blood. Track worked open the seat restraints and Emilio's eyes opened.

Track hauled the man from the cockpit and aft, toward the fuselage door. Flames were licking from the electrical wiring now.

Emilio sagged against him, and Track scanned the aft compartment—if there was a fourth life vest he couldn't see it. Track shrugged out of his own vest, getting it around Emilio, inflating it, and then hurling the Mexican into the waves. Track dived after him.

He tugged at Emilio. The waves were higher than Track had thought, and flames lashed from the open fuselage door. Swimming away from the wreck, Track held the Mexican's head above the water, towing him.

He felt its impact before he heard or saw it, and he dragged Emilio beneath the waves.

The helicopter was gone, fire and a rain of burning debris all that was left as Track surfaced again, spitting saltwater, hauling the choking Emilio with him.

Bobbing in the water nearby he could see Miles Jefferson. George was off to Track's left, waving his Jack Daniels cap.

Track looked around them. He could see the supertanker ahead, perhaps a quarter mile away.

There was nothing else on the water.

George shouted, laughing, "A fine mess you've gotten us into this time—hmm!"

"Shove it," Track snapped back.

But then Track could hear something very faintly. He looked up. Rising from the deck of the supertanker was something that looked like a massive insect. He stared at it until he had to blink—then he stared at it again as it rose. He heard the unmistakable growl of rotor noise.

"Hey—they're going to rescue us!" Track exclaimed, looking toward his nephew.

"And leave a congressman to float around in the damn ocean? They sure better rescue us!"

Track looked at Emilio. The man very feebly moved his right hand up from the water and made the sign of the cross, whispering, *"¡Madre de Dios!"*

Track held the man's chin up as the helicopter angled toward them, and he whispered, "I'm with you, pal."

But a thought was already nagging at the back of Track's mind as the chopper hovered over them and the water swirled up around them—who was the Master of D.E.A.T.H.? Somehow he had a feeling he'd find out, and he wouldn't like it at all.

MORE GREAT ACTION COMING SOON

When there's no one else to turn to!

#8 Revenge of the Master by Jerry Ahern

With the future of the U.S. space program in the balance, two orbiting space shuttles are preparing to deploy a valuable cargo high above the Earth.

But a power-mad, evil genius is planning an explosive episode that will bring U.S. space exploration to a brutal and disastrous end—unless the right man can be found to stop him.

In a tale of high adventure on the new frontier, Dan Track once again battles an old enemy when he comes up against the leader of the criminal syndicate known as D.E.A.T.H.

This is the crisis everyone said couldn't happen. Now it has.

Track is Explosive!